JEROME
A Ghost Story

GARY LEE VINCENT

Burning Bulb
PUBLISHING

Jerome
By **Gary Lee Vincent**

Burning Bulb Publishing
P.O. Box 4721
Bridgeport, WV 26330-4721
United States of America
www.BurningBulbPublishing.com

Cover designed by Melissa St. Giles.

First Edition.

Paperback Edition ISBN: 978-1-948278-59-1

Also by Gary Lee Vincent

Novels
PASSAGEWAY
BELLY TIMBER
ATTACK OF THE MELONHEADS
WHEN THE BEDPOSTS SHAKE (RING OF THE SUCCUBUS)
IMPOUND
STRANGE FRIENDS
THE BEST ACTORS THAT EVER LIVED
THE BLIND MELODY

Darkened—The West Virginia Vampire Series
DARKENED HILLS
DARKENED HOLLOWS
DARKENED WATERS
DARKENED SOULS
DARKENED MINDS
DARKENED DESTINIES

The Douglas River Vampire Series
RIVER: A VAMPIRE'S NIGHTMARE
ICARUS

The Black Circle Chronicles
PROVE YOUR LOVE
STRANGE NEW POWERS
NIGHT WINGS
SHEEP AMONGST WOLVES
LORD OF THE BIRDS

Dedicated to
Julie Michelle McCullough

CHAPTER 1

It was late evening and Herman Broderick was once more trying to watch television in his hotel room at the Jerome Grand Hotel, but just like on his previous attempts, the TV signal was bad.

Herman, who'd checked into the Jerome Grand Hotel yesterday, scowled at the television. This was simply unacceptable. So far, he must have tried a hundred different cable channels to no avail. No news, no soaps or reality shows, no sports or fishing shows, no TCM or other movie channels . . .

The internet television channels were behaving exactly the same; meaning no Netflix either.

It wasn't that the TV showed no pictures at all, but that the pictures came and went like the wind.

Herman would get a ghost of a picture, but it would look washed out like a shirt passed through soapy water too many times; and the TV sound would be half speech and half static, practically white noise that set Herman's teeth on edge. But even this distorted visual wouldn't last very long. Just as quickly as the washed-out image had stabilized on the screen, it was suddenly gone again, converting into a mess of wavy horizontal lines, which then converted to a full-blown pepper-salt static visual, accompanied by crackling static noise if Herman was unwise enough to leave the sound on. (He'd made that mistake a few times already, when he'd temporarily gotten a halfway decent picture; but once the shifty images had faded away and he'd been left with the noise, he'd always regretted his actions. He'd wised up now and just left the sound off while doing his futile channel surfing.)

Herman was finding it frustrating as hell. He kept pointing the remote at the offending TV and stabbing it with his finger in the hope that something somewhere would reach through to the television from Cable-TV-Land.

After what had to be Herman's hundredth futile attempt to find a station with decent reception, he quit. He'd been defeated. In ordinary circumstances, the logical thing to do if presented with a hotel room where the amenities didn't work, was to call reception and lodge a complaint about the misbehaving TV, and demand a new room.

But in this case, no!

Herman sighed. Then he walked over to the hotel cordless on the coffee table and picked it up. He pressed the '0' button for 'reception,' and placed the receiver to his ear. He heard no ringing at the other end. He pulled the phone away from his ear, disconnected the call and then redialed. Once more he heard silence in the earpiece. No, not silence; there was a sound, a whirling sort of sound. It was like the static noise from the TV, but at much lower volume.

Same as yesterday, then.

He stared back over at the TV again, which was busy replacing a washed-out image of a middle-aged woman with bluish static.

Herman scowled and dropped the receiver back into its cradle. *This is ludicrous; at least the telephone should work.*

But he was flogging a dead horse. The telephone hadn't worked since he'd checked in here.

The Jerome Grand Hotel came highly recommended. Well, it did, if one overlooked the creepy stories that were associated with the building. But if one was bothered by creepy stuff, what was one doing here in Jerome in the first place? The whole town was supposedly a creep show.

Herman Broderick was a reasonable man; he'd not let any of the ridiculous rumors bother him. He'd made a reservation at the hotel partly on the recommendation of his friends and partly because he'd known Nancy would love the place.

Thinking of Nancy Lee brought a broad smile to Herman's face. He wondered how she was feeling. *Her darn TV and telephone don't work either so I'm sure she's bored as hell too!*

Herman and Nancy had driven over together from the neighboring town of Black Canyon, where they both lived. She was in the room next door. He and she had spent the morning together, but then, a short while ago, Nancy had complained of a headache and said she felt like taking a nap.

Herman wished there was a connecting door between their rooms, then he sighed. Not yet, not yet. But hopefully soon.

The malfunctioning media equipment made him feel frustrated. The only solution would be to head down to reception and make a complaint. Which would possibly result, if the hotel had a room where both TV and phone *did* work, in Herman being moved to another room. The problem with this was that, as far as Herman could tell, all of the other hotel rooms on this floor were taken, which meant he would most like be moved to a room on another floor.

Seeing as moving from this room would likely mean that Nancy Lee would no longer be close by, Herman decided to tough it out for another day or two, before complaining. The malfunctioning multimedia equipment had one positive side to it. It provided him with a great excuse to spend more time with Nancy, both inside and outside of her hotel room.

Herman grinned at the thought: *Seeing as we'll both be getting bored on a regular basis, best to experience that boredom together.*

And, crap telecoms or not, the view from up here was great.

Herman got up from his chair and made his way out through the glass balcony door, onto the balcony of his 'valley-side' room. Once outside, he instinctively cast a glance sideways to his right, imagining as he stared at the intervening wall, that he could see the balcony door to the next room, where Nancy Lee lay sweetly slumbering. Then, grinning to himself from sweet thoughts of her, Herman returned his attention to his surroundings.

The Jerome Grand Hotel was a five-story Spanish mission-style building that was originally built in the early twentieth century as the United Verde Hospital, and which occupied the highest point in the Verde Valley, from which it presided over the town of Jerome.

Herman was rooming up on the fourth floor of the Jerome Grand Hotel, and from here was afforded a panoramic view of the area; the cloudy blue sky and the hilly Arizona countryside with its shrub-like vegetation and its rises and dips.

Directly below him lay the hotel parking lot, and beyond and below the parking lot, lay the town of Jerome itself.

The entire town was built up near the top of Mingus Mountain, set in a descending mountainside slope that was serviced by Arizona's State Route 89A.

Jerome, Arizona, wasn't a large town. At the moment, it boasted a population of around four hundred people, mostly artists and musicians. The town did however have historical significance in both county and state, as well as a kind of paranormal notoriety, both of which made it a tourist spot, with most of the visitors coming to experience the town's supposed ghosts for themselves.

But Herman Broderick didn't believe in ghosts.

This quaint tourist trap of nowadays was a far cry from the town's heyday a little over a century ago, when Jerome had been a thriving copper mining spot. Back then the town had had a population of fifteen thousand; miners, traders . . . and of course prostitutes, to comfort the miners. Back then, so much vice had apparently happened in this small town that it had earned Jerome the title of the 'Wickedest City in the West,' as declared by a New York newspaper.

After a while, Herman got tired of standing out on the balcony, and staring at the town below and at the countryside around it.

Suddenly, he felt that age had begun telling on him. No, his mind wasn't weakening on him, though he'd be the first to admit that his thinking was slowing down. He wasn't anywhere near as fit as he'd been on his fortieth birthday, five years ago.

He walked back into his hotel room.

Try as he might Herman couldn't get Nancy Lee out of his mind for long. He was really looking forward to seeing her tonight.

CHAPTER 2

"Ah yes, finally I got you suckers," Earl Roche thought with glee.

Just to make perfectly certain of what he now had on record, Earl replayed the digital sound file. Since capturing it, he'd transferred the recording to an audio editing program on his laptop, so that now as it played back again, he saw both a waveform representation and a spectrogram of the noises.

He smiled to himself as the sounds reemerged from his top-of-the-range loudspeakers. First though, there was silence which lasted for about twenty seconds. Feeling impatient to get into the nitty-gritty of things, Earl scrolled forward through the sound file. There was no chance of him missing his target noises—they stood out loud and proud in the translated waveform map. He stopped scrolling two seconds before his desired noises happened.

They happened. First was the sound of a door opening. Then then the door closed again and afterwards came the dulled thud of footsteps briskly crossing the room. Then he heard a woman's voice sighing, then came the sound of her body settling itself down on a chair and then a cat meowing; and then . . . silence.

Not much unusual about any of that of course, except that in this case, the recording had been made in the middle of the night in an empty room. What Earl had captured with his recording equipment was the sound of a ghost.

Hearing that short sequence of sounds, which actually lasted less than fifteen seconds, raised the hairs on the back of Earl's thick neck and cause a shiver to run down his spine.

Earl grinned to himself and then he laughed. Finally, he'd gotten conclusive proof that this darn Jerome Grand Hotel was haunted.

I've finally accomplished it! I'm the first. I'll be famous.

But then his exhilaration faded. He shut off the sound file, which was now playing a routine low-volume hum into the room, got up from his chair, and paced about in some frustration.

But what have I captured actually? Who was that up there last night? The nurse? The woman in white who sometimes appears near the elevator? Or . . . or are Keith and Minnie simply playing a gag on me? I wouldn't put it past those two to have some fun at my expense.

His expression soured and he walked over to the window and stared out at the balcony, from which a warm evening breeze was making its way into the hotel room.

No, Earl Roche didn't doubt that his brother and his brother's girlfriend could trick him just for the fun of it—it would be easy enough for Keith to bribe a spare key to Room 32 out of the receptionist and then for him to slip Minnie in there at 2 a.m. to fake the sounds that Earl had just heard.

But even that wasn't the true cause of Earl's frustration. To be honest to himself, Earl was certain his slacker brother hadn't pulled any shenanigans of that sort. The recording sounded genuine, there was something raw and unfeigned about the way the woman in the audio recording had entered the room, crossed it and sat down. *And besides . . . if that was Minnie playing a trick, why didn't I hear her leaving the room afterwards?*

Earl sighed as the logical answer to that question came to his mind: *Because Keith erased the recording beyond that point. I didn't think to set it to voice-activated mode. If only I could record video, then I'd know for sure!*

But video recording was the sticking point here. As far as Earl had been able to determine, recording video in any of the reputedly haunted parts of this building never worked. Here in his room he could film away as much as he liked and the camera captured everything, and the same applied to the hotel lobby downstairs and parts of the stairways. But once he took his gear out to any of the supposedly psychically charged places in the Jerome Grand Hotel, he came away with nothing.

Hoping against hope that he'd succeed where others had failed, last night Earl had set up two infrared video cameras in Room 32, by reputation one of the most haunted rooms in this building. Both cameras had created blank files for him.

And without any video to back up his creepy sound file . . .

Dammit! If I am unsure of what I'm listening to—if I am thinking I'm being pranked—what do I expect the general public, not to mention our ghost-hunting competitors to think about the recording? Those guys and girls have seen and heard all kinds of faked 'captures,' including professionally done special effects fakery that makes Paranormal Activity look like Ghostbusters. No one in their right mind will take what I've got on tape seriously.

Earl sighed and sat down again.

***

Earl Roche was thirty-five, and looked every inch the nerd he was; a pudgy nondescript bearded guy. He worked a day job as a junior bank manager; and while managing other people's money for eight hours at a stretch was boring as hell, the bank job more than compensated Earl by paying for the expensive equipment he required for his life's true passion, which was ghost-hunting.

Together with his younger brother Keith, Earl had set up Paranormal Research Brothers, and over the past few years the organization had slowly but surely gained a reputation for accurate research into spooky activity not just here in the Grand Canyon State, but the entire American southwest. Of course, working the bank job meant that Earl only had weekends and holidays/vacations to really devote to his passion, but he had always been certain that given sufficient time, he'd hit on something big, something that would gain him national recognition and possibly enable him quit his day job to instead work on paranormal shows for television, which was a lifelong dream of his.

But PRB hadn't yet scored with that big scoop, and so for the moment Earl had to be content with hosting the Paranormal Research

Brothers' weekly YouTube show, and also being consulted by those in the know of his reliability when the authenticity of a spooky recording was in doubt.

Earl was on vacation now, which was why he'd come here. For ghosthunters, this old town of Jerome had the reputation of being the motherlode, much like it had had been for copper when it was a mining town. Here there were reputedly ghosts on every street corner and in every old house. Earl had researched exhaustively on the town of Jerome before loading the necessary PRB equipment into their van and heading over here with Keith and Minnie. As far as he could tell, most of the info on this place was legit; Jerome had ghosts to spare. Which begged the question, where were they hiding?

Earl had booked rooms for his research crew at the Jerome Grand Hotel because of its famous 'resident ghosts,' but so far, he'd seen none of them. Which was frustrating, since he'd already spent a week of his vacation and had just four days left.

And so yesterday, I booked Room 32 for the night. I got lucky there; the dude with the reservation cancelled at the last minute. I might try again in 32 if there's any other vacant slots this week, but without video . . . it'll likely add up to a waste of money. But so far, other than those cat footprints I think I found on my bed the day after we arrived . . . I've gotten nada for the money invested in this. Oh, screw the money—that's not the important thing! I don't care how much it costs! I just need results!

He heard a knock on his door. After walking over and peeking through the peephole, he let Keith and Minnie into the room.

While Earl took after his father in looks, his brother took after their mother. Thirty-two-year-old Keith Roche was tall and muscular and good-looking. He was a painter, but lacked the motivation to really claw his way up through the art world; or to excel in any profession really. Keith was just a slacker.

Most of the time Keith was broke and sponged off Earl. Earl put up with this because he needed someone to keep an eye on their paranormal setup while he was busy with his nine-to-five; and also needed help with his investigations. As irresponsible as Keith was, he could at least set up cameras; and his expertise with colors sometimes proved invaluable to their research. Earl wasn't married and also had no girlfriend, and so he could afford the extra cost of Keith's generally empty wallet. Just like he could afford the pay Minnie Connors for her assistance.

Keith's girlfriend for the past three years, Minnie, was petite and pretty. She was twenty-seven. Minnie acted as anchorwoman for their PRB broadcasts. Earl both lacked the look of a television personality and also had no confidence in front of a camera, except if he was being interviewed or explaining something technical. Keith on the other hand, had the looks, but tended to be mic-shy, he could never think of what to say. Earl had initially intended to pair Keith and Minnie as anchorpersons, but even when handed a script, Keith would flub his lines, so Earl had had to let that idea go to the waste bin.

"I hate how we can't get proper internet reception in here," Minnie said, waving her phone in the air after she'd sat down opposite the television. "This is a scam, we were promised great Wi-Fi, and yet—"

"I think we caught something last night," Earl said.

As he'd expected, his comment immediately silenced Minnie, who might otherwise have gone on bemoaning the general deplorable state of telecoms in this hotel. Minnie Connors was a very nice girl in lots of ways, but she got irritated easily. At least it seemed that way to Earl, who'd always had difficulty figuring women out, which was part of the reason why at age thirty-five he was still single and his last serious relationship with a woman had occurred three years ago.

Not so Keith. Keith just ignored Minnie when she got her moods, which, as far as Earl could tell, she either didn't mind or didn't notice. More evidence for him that he'd never understand women.

While Minnie had been making herself comfortable on Earl's bed, Keith had raided the icebox for beers. After taking out two for himself and Minnie, he looked at Earl with a raised eyebrow. Earl nodded; Keith extracted a third beer from the icebox, then passed them around.

"We caught something on film?" Keith asked. "We finally got video?"

Earl shook his head. "Just audio. But there's no mistaking what it was."

He clicked on the laptop screen and replayed what they'd recorded. He and Keith had both collected the infrared cameras and other recording equipment from Room 32 this morning, but there had been hours of recorded data to work through, and as Keith didn't have the patience for that, Earl had done the job himself.

Earl regarded his two companions as they listened to the sounds of the door opening and then shutting again, the muffled footsteps, and finally the feminine sigh and cat meow. Keith was listening closely to everything with a kind of amusement on his face; Earl still wondered if his brother thought the whole PRB thing was a lark. There was however no mistaking Minnie's response to the recording. She'd been listening placidly, and showing little interest too, but then, right when the cat meowed, all of a sudden Minnie looked scared; her eyes spread wide open and she began breathing fast, while looking like she was about to drop her bottle of beer and flee from the room.

Keith too had noticed her reaction. "Relax, baby, it can't hurt us," he told her gently.

She nodded quickly. "Sure, it can't. But don't you ask me to accompany you back to that horrible room again."

Earl smiled. "That's alright; we won't." He felt some relief. She clearly wasn't faking her fright, which just as clearly meant that the recording was genuine; she and Keith hadn't pulled a prank on him.

For a moment, the depth of Minnie's fright bothered Earl. Yes, she was rather timid—he knew that the main reason she did the shows with them was because she was madly in love with Keith and didn't want another woman snatching him away from her under the pretext of working together—but this wasn't the first time that Minnie had been faced with something preternatural. Despite her fears of the not-quite-dead they researched, she'd always traveled with them to each site they'd visited. She was a trooper, that was for sure; and she'd endured some rather chilling situations quite well.

And yet, now, for some reason, all the color was draining from her face.

"Well, I'll admit its creepy, that's for sure," Keith said. "Spookiest thing I've heard in quite a while. Gave me shivers down my spine." Then he noticed that Minnie was shivering and walked over to sit beside her. "You okay, baby?" he asked after wrapping his arm around her shoulder. "Forgive me for saying it, but you look like you just seen a you-know-what."

Minnie snuggled up close to him. "I don't know, Keith. This place, this hotel . . ." she pointed at the laptop. "Those sounds. I don't know!"

Keith hugged her closer and looked at Earl. "So, what now, bro?"

Earl frowned. "We need video," he said fiercely. "There's been all sort of tales about this town and this hotel, but as in all ghost tales, it's just another story if we can't show the spooks going about their business."

While saying this, Earl had directed the attention of his companions to their array of ghost-hunting gear neatly arranged in boxes in the left corner of his room.

There were EMF/electromagnetic readers designed to detect even the most minute amounts of unusual radiation; a special radio that cycled through hundreds of frequency bands with a view to picking up disturbances in the ghostly ether; the regular Ouija boards for directly contacting the spirits of the dead; and also two special cameras, which used infrared vision to see in the dark and hopefully photograph what haunted the Jerome Grand Hotel. Whatever stuff Earl hadn't found space for in here was kept across the hall in Minnie and Keith's room; more esoteric gear, and more Ouija boards.

So far, using the Ouija boards had proved a spectacular failure.

"I agree with Earl that video is important," Minnie said, with a shudder.

Keith sipped his beer. "Been done before, baby. I mean filming spooks. No one believed them either—claimed they were special effects."

Earl nodded. "I know, I know. But there has to be a way to do it credibly. I just need time to figure this out. Unfortunately, my vacation time might run out before I crack this."

While Keith comforted Minnie, Earl Roche drank his beer and pondered the knotty problem of how to catch a ghost on camera, in a building where cameras mostly didn't work on ghosts.

"Well, first off," he said after a while, "We know for a fact that the reason the cameras don't record is the same reason that the cells don't work."

"No, we don't know that for a fact," Minnie said, having recovered her composure in the interim. "We're just theorizing and assuming there. There could be something completely different messing up the camera recordings."

Earl nodded slowly. "Alright, I can agree with that." He looked at his brother. "You got any ideas how we can skirt around this roadblock?"

Keith shook his head. "Nah, bro, but let's just keep drinkin' and thinkin', and I'm sure we'll figure something out."

CHAPTER 3

Nancy Lee was fifty-three. She'd been widowed at age fifty, when her husband Micah Lee had suddenly slumped forward into his spaghetti dinner. The years since then had been a bit rough emotionally, but Nancy had survived, just like most people did in similar situations. But for her, survival was subsistence-level existence; Nancy wanted to live, live, live; and enjoy the life she was living.

Nancy was a standup comedienne. Naturally funny and quite talented and successful, she toured the country on a regular basis, performing at The Hollywood Improv in Los Angeles and the Comedy Cellar in NYC. Her late husband Micah had been both her manager and her traveling partner for twenty years, and this had made his death a double loss. Nowadays, their daughter Harriet handled Nancy's bookings. Sure, the gal did an admirable job, but she was no traveling companion. Harriet had a husband and kids of her own and had let Nancy know that her family was her priority; she wasn't about leaving them to shepherd her mother across the United States.

Nancy understood; in her youth she'd have done exactly the same thing.

So now Nancy either traveled by road in the company of friends or flew to her engagements. However one looked at it though, it was still a lonely life she led, not the kind of life Nancy had envisaged for herself in middle-age.

But all that had changed a month ago, when she'd reconnected with Herman Broderick on Facebook. A little conversation quickly revealed that just like herself, Herman was now single again; although in his case the reason for his Facebook profile reading 'Single/Not in a relationship with anyone' was divorce, not death.

Nancy had wondered which was worse. Was it better for the loved one to become a no-longer-loved one, or was it better for them to transition to a (hopefully) better place?

Nancy vaguely recalled Herman's ex-wife Louise, a small, shrewish woman with a razor-sharp tongue. How Herman had ever fallen in love with Louise, not to mention married her, had never ceased to amaze Nancy. Once she'd realized how much of a caustic spirit Louise Broderick possessed, Nancy had kept as far away from her as she could. Which meant she'd seen Herman less and less over the years.

In any case, what was important was that Herman was single again and once she'd realized that he still found her attractive, Nancy had decided it was time to move on with her life; hopefully with Herman in her corner.

This would be the second time they'd dated. The first time had been twenty years ago. Herman had just begun working as a real estate agent then, while Nancy had just regional stand-up tour. They'd met at an after-performance party of hers and something had clicked between them. It hadn't lasted though. Possibly because she was older than him—back then, the eight-year difference in their ages had seemed more like eight hundred—and possibly because her touring schedule had resulted in her never being around Phoenix (or his neck of the woods, Black Canyon) for him to romance her; unlike comediennes, real estate agents didn't go on tour.

On a proper retrospective analysis, Nancy had realized that the second possible reason for the failure of their fledgling romance was the true one. Her tour manager for that very first tour had been Micah Lee, whom she had soon fallen in love with and married.

And now twenty years have rushed by like water flushed down a drain and both Micah and Louise are no longer a part of our lives. Herman and I are both back exactly where we started from. Viewed from a logical perspective, things might have worked out better if we'd just gotten married to each other back then. We'd very likely still be together. And we're both older too—we both look like prunes. When I introduced him to Harriet, she thought he was older than I was!

Nancy sighed and wondered why her television hardly ever worked. And yet, she apparently got better reception than Herman did. Herman was eternally in here to stare at the messy images onscreen. Apparently, this was the case all over Jerome—television signals were crappy, with the stated reason being something to do with the old copper deposits in the hills messing up reception. That was the way the bartender had explained it anyway. According to him, the loss of signal wasn't permanent, it waxed and waned, determined by whatever arcane magnetic forces controlled such things. But the signal blackout could sometimes last for days.

Nancy didn't believe this however. Earlier today—when she and Herman had gone out sightseeing—she'd heard the sound of television programs coming from the other rooms. She intended to discuss this with Herman. whom she expected would be knocking on her door in a short while.

In the interim, Nancy got out her compact mirror from her purse and examined her face. Gray eyes, framed by long blond hair with just a hint of gray in it. Frowning, she explored the skin at the corner of her eyes with her fingers.

Ah, the crow's feet have returned from their migratory travels, she thought in amusement. *Maybe it's time to have that damn facelift I've been putting off forever. All the other girls have had one—if I'm not careful, I'll end up looking like their mother.* She laughed. *Still I don't look too bad for my age. At least Herman doesn't think I do. He can't seem to get enough of me!*

This was flattering in the extreme, and yet Nancy still felt that intense vulnerability all women develop with age. Despite their reunion, Herman still hadn't kissed her yet. Meaning, he hadn't yet kissed her on the lips like a lover: those cute cheek kisses he kept giving her didn't count. It was frustrating! She wanted Herman to kiss her properly. She wanted to belong to him again, like she had all those long years ago. And she knew he felt the same way towards her. She kept noticing him from the corner of her eye, saw him watching her when he thought she wasn't looking at him, saw his lips moving hesitantly like he had something on the tip of his tongue, that he had to tell her, if he could just find the courage.

Nancy replaced the mirror in her purse and got to her feet in a fit of irritation.

Herman needs to find his damn courage quickly. I'm getting very tired of sleeping alone every night! I need Herman's arms around me when I'm sleeping. I want to wake up wrapped in his arms each morning.

Still feeling slightly angry that her seducer wasn't seducing her fast enough, Nancy walked out onto her balcony and looked out over the town.

For some reason, what Nancy saw out there depressed her. However, for the life of her, she couldn't explain what the trouble with the view was. It was quaint, with just the right mix of old and new buildings to prevent the town being considered another southern museum, and yet . . . it troubled her. It really did.

There's something really wrong with this place, she thought. *I would love to be able to figure out what it is. Or . . . or . . . is it all that silly talk of ghosts yesterday getting to me?*

The 'silly talk of ghosts' hadn't been intentional. While waiting for Herman in the hotel bar, Nancy had met a bookish young man in there. He'd recognized her from TV and had engaged her in conversation. It turned out he was some kind of ghosthunter.

For a moment even that description chilled her. 'Ghosthunter' sounded eerily close to 'witch hunter'—she had a vision of that slightly plump and bearded young man dressed in eighteenth century getup, with a three-cornered hat atop his head, placing a burning torch against a pile of sticks arranged around the feet of some nubile young woman, who screamed piteously while she subsequently burnt to death.

But in truth, the young man—Earl, she recalled his first name was, though his surname had by now fled her mind—had been pleasing enough. It turned out that he was also rooming here in the hotel, also on this third floor. Herman had however arrived before the young man could properly explain how he and his two friends expected to film the ghosts that they found here.

He had however spooked her a little by then; particularly his talk of this hotel being haunted.

Of course, just like everyone else in Arizona, Nancy was familiar with the tales about Jerome, how, if the stories were to believed, it was haunted like no other place on Earth. But she for one had never given much credence to tales of ghosts. Nancy had traveled too widely, was too cosmopolitan, to believe in spooks; and yet . . . at the moment 'spooked' was the only accurate description for how she felt.

Of course, Nancy Lee realized that part of the trouble she was having with accepting Jerome as a normal place was that it was an actual 'ghost town,' not in the sense of it having ghosts, but rather that of it having been deserted through the passage of years.

This place hardly has any resident population and a few tourists aren't exactly gonna be filling up the streets, are they?

She looked down at an old negro man in the parking lot and wondered if he was real or not.

Of course, he's real, you dimwit, he's as real as you are!

Feeling angry with herself for being so impressionable, Nancy shut her eyes firmly and dug her fingernails deeply into her palms, anything to 'unspook' herself.

When she opened her eyes again, the old man was gone.

But was he ever really there at all? Or rather, what sort of existence had he had? Had he merely turned the corner up ahead and so walked out of sight in a normal way? Or . . . had he instead turned and walked through a wall?

Thinking it had to be the former and hoping it wasn't actually the latter, Nancy returned to her room.

She was delivered from her upsetting reverie by the sound of Herman knocking on the door of her hotel room. Even then, the sound flustered her for a moment. Well, it had to be Herman (whom she now occasionally thought of as 'her man'). But what if it wasn't him? What if it was one of those 'things' knocking? What if when she opened her door, she found not Herman Broderick standing outside of her room, but rather a ghost, like that young man Earl had suggested she might?

Either I'm getting old or the heat is getting to me, she thought with a grimace at the slowly turning fan overhead. It was May and the weather was quite hot.

Nancy got over her fears and hurried to open the door before Herman either concluded that she was still asleep and went downstairs without her, or worse yet, grew scared that something had happened to her and called 911, though he'd have to leave the hotel to get a phone signal.

Though she knew it couldn't be anyone else out there, she was relieved to see that it actually was Herman. In an uncharacteristic move since he'd reappeared in her life, she stepped up close to him and hugged him. Then, realizing how much out of character she must seem, she quickly stepped back and tried not to look sheepish.

Her hug had apparently startled him too. He didn't seem to mind though. Instead, he seemed pleased, but was doing his best not to appear too eager.

"You look a bit worried," he said as he stepped into the room. "Did anything happen that you want to tell me about?"

"Bad dream," she quickly replied. "Something about this hotel room—or maybe it's this whole building that's feeding my subconscious with nightmares." She shuddered. "Hold on, while I fetch my purse. I'm gonna need a few drinks to settle myself again."

CHAPTER 4

After a short while of listening to Earl and Keith discussing the kind of supernatural trap they could rig to catch one of the Jerome Hotel's ghosts on film, Minnie excused herself, telling the brothers that she needed to rest a bit.

But in truth, Minnie's problem wasn't that she needed to rest, but that if Earl played that creepy recording one more time in her hearing today, she was certain she'd go mad from fright.

I already think I'm going mad!

The brothers were too engrossed in their talk of magnetic force fields and degaussers and other technical stuff to notice the agitated look on Minnie's face as she got up from the bed and made her way over to the front door.

At the door she looked back into the room and forced a smile when Keith blew her a kiss. Then she was outside of Earl's room and crossing the hallway to the opposite door, and shortly stepping into the sanctuary of the room she shared with Keith.

Once inside their room, Minnie hurried through to the bedroom area and flung herself down on the bed. Then she rolled over and stared at the ceiling, while fear filled her.

I'm not going mad then! She thought. I didn't imagine what happened yesterday! I really did see that cat!

***

Just like she'd just done, yesterday evening Minnie had excused herself from sitting in with the Roche brothers while they finalized how they would wire up Room 32 to catch impressions of the ghosts that were said to haunt it.

Yesterday however, Minnie's motivation to depart from Earl's room hadn't been fear, but rather exhaustion. She had spent a good part of the afternoon window-shopping at the quaint shops on Main Street, and felt justifiably tired and wanted to rest for a while before they went down to the bar. At the moment Earl and Keith spent a lot of time drinking at the hotel bar; and Minnie generally went where Keith went, which meant she spent a lot of time drinking at that same bar too.

She thought it a wonder that none of them ever got drunk enough to make a fool of themselves. Their revelry generally ended in them singing extracts from civil war songs cussing the 'damn yankees,' in which any other bar crawlers tended to join in, even those visitors from the northern states of the federation.

The barkeep must be watering everyone's drinks, Minnie had decided.

***

Minnie Connors was originally from New Braunfels, Texas. She'd moved to Tucson, Arizona after finishing high school and not finding any jobs she liked in her hometown. In Tucson, she'd waitressed, worked as a Walmart cashier, and also been a pizza delivery girl, which was how she'd met Earl and Keith, driving up to their place on her motorcycle at 9 p.m., and finding herself both bemused by the amount of weird mechanical devices stocked in Earl's living room and by how handsome his younger brother was. The 'younger brother' was just as taken with her apparently and managed to get her phone number before paying the pizza bill.

Fast forward three years, and now Minnie and Keith were an inseparable item. She'd thought it only natural to join Earl's ghost-hunting team, and had been pleased to discover that she was a natural on camera.

Truth be told, Minnie Connors knew that she was a scaredy-cat. Chasing ghosts around the state of Arizona had never been her idea of fun; like most young women her age, she preferred going to the cinema, attending parties, and clubbing. But Keith was committed to his brother's paranormal research, and Minnie understood that if she wanted to see as much of Keith as possible, she needed to commit to the Paranormal Research Bros too. Earl paid them both—she more than Keith, who lived with him anyway—and that extra money helped a lot with her expenses, when combined with her barely-above-minimum-wage salary from her succession of jobs.

***

So, yesterday afternoon, Minnie had taken her well-deserved nap. She'd woken up at a little past five o'clock with the strange feeling that she wasn't alone in she and Keith's room. Looking around, she'd discovered that her suspicions were correct. There was a large black cat standing on the dresser.

The cat, which was sleek and well-groomed, had been staring at itself in the dresser mirror. Minnie's initial impression on seeing it had been surprise and not fear. She'd had no idea how it could have gotten into the hotel room, as all of the windows were shut because the AC unit was working.

"Hey, kitty, kitty, over here!" she'd nonetheless called out to the cat.

The animal had turned towards the sound of her voice and then leapt from the dresser to the dresser stool and finally across onto the bed. On reaching the bed, the cat had calmly walked up to Minnie's side, then had sat on her stomach and looked at her.

Minnie had instinctively reached down a hand to stroke it, and oddly enough, that was when her fear had set in. On touching the black feline, she'd felt something inexpressible in words emanating from the beast. She'd stared at it and it stared back at her. Its green eyes projected not malice but curiosity. Minnie had the definite impression that the cat was surprised to find her in here. Which, considering that she was the guest and the black cat the intruder, was a strange feeling indeed to have. But this absurd exchange of territorial roles paled into insignificance against the sheer weight of the terror that filled her while she stroked the cat.

Then, she had felt very uneasy as a chill came upon her, like some unknown terror was causing her skin to itch all over at the same time. Her heart began racing. *Was she going to die?* Gooseflesh broke out all over her body.

Minnie couldn't understand it at all, but so long as she was in contact with the creature, she'd had that understanding; that this harmless-seeming black animal represented her death. And not just hers, but that of Keith and Earl also.

This is so preposterous, she had thought, and had stopped stroking the cat. The cat seeming took no offense to her withdrawal of her affections. Instead it got down from her belly and meowed at her, while rubbing itself against her left arm. It was a loud meow for sure, and one that had an unusual ring to it. The eerie feline noise seemed to fill the room and it put Minnie's nerves on edge. And once again she'd felt dread of the creature and had the sense of its presence presaging her death and that of her two male companions.

And in addition, she had had the silly feeling that she knew this cat from somewhere; that she and it were in some way acquainted.

She had lain there in bed, seemingly unable to move. The cat had rubbed against her arm, and had purred happily; and the tension between it and Minnie had grown and grown . . .

But then, the noise of the suite door clicking open had saved Minnie from . . . she hadn't known what was about to happen, just that if it had happened it would have probably been terrible indeed.

She had looked out into the corridor and had seen Keith stepping inside their room. Then she had looked away from him to the cat again, intending to draw his attention to the animal's presence in their suite.

But the cat was no longer seated beside her on the bed. Nor (as it turned out after some surreptitious investigation on Minnie's part), was it anywhere in the room anymore.

Apparently, the creature had been a ghost. That had scared Minnie. She'd wanted to immediately tell Keith about her experience, but Keith had been in a hurry. He'd only come into their room to get a reel of duct tape that Earl needed from a suitcase. He'd kissed Minnie and been gone again before she could say a word about their feline visitor.

Despite the length of time that she had worked with both Keith and his older brother, Minnie still worried that her boyfriend would laugh at her if she told him of the weird sense of death that the cat ghost had communicated to her when she had touched it.

And Minnie Connors had something else she wanted to discuss with Keith, something of vital importance to their relationship, that wasn't a laughing matter at all. She had intended to call Keith aside after dinner so they could have a private heart-to-heart discussion about their future, but her experience with the ghost cat had completely destroyed every feeling of a romantic mood that had been building in her.

So yesterday, Minnie had thrown her romantic plans out of the window. And of course, as the evening had progressed, and she and the two men had later descended to the bar for some drunken reverie, the afternoon's chilling impressions of terror had quickly dissolved into alcoholic haze, and had mentioning the black cat to her companions had become much less important with each glass of wine she had consumed, until, by the time that Minnie had woken up this morning, the whole thing had seemed utterly silly to her.

But that indifference had of course ended when Earl had played the creepy recording he'd made last night in Room 32.

Because the eerie meow that had concluded the recording was exactly the same one as the cat had made while laying against her body.

Minnie was certain of it. Yes, she knew there were millions of cats in the USA, possibly even in Arizona, too. But to her, at least, the eerie sound of that miserable meow could only have come from that black ghost cat she'd seen.

CHAPTER 5

Earl Roche was finding it hard to contain his excitement, which was now increasing by leaps and bounds. Totally out of the blue, he realized he had made a discovery, one that might further his research into the ghosts of Jerome, Arizona.

Earl got to his feet and got a fresh beer out of the icebox. He was however aware that he'd not come to Jerome to win the Arizonan grand prize for drunkenness, but to extend the reaches of paranormal research.

That stated, he twisted the top off of the beer bottle and got down to drinking it. He tried the TV again, discovered it was more of the same nothing, and once more turned it off and cast the remote control aside on the bed.

The weird thing about the supposedly tenuous nature of the hotel's phone and television connections was how inconsistent they appeared to be.

Minnie, who was a television addict, swore that just this morning, while making her way along their corridor en route to the elevator, she'd heard TV broadcasts from three hotel rooms. Minnie had said that she hadn't at first been convinced of what she was hearing; so she'd actually stood by each door for a while to make certain her ears weren't deceiving her. And furthermore, when she'd gotten downstairs, the TV in the bar had been working, broadcasting a CNN report about Covid-19 in Asia.

"But I can't even get the Fashion Channel!" Minnie had complained, to which Earl had nodded understandingly, and replied, "I share your pain. Even though I'm in no way athletic myself, I like to follow the NFL. That's been a total no-no since our arrival here."

Then he'd remembered something: "Hey, you said you were gonna call your brother from the public library. How'd that work out?"

Minnie had shaken her head and looked very pissed off. "It didn't. Would you believe that I forgot my phone here in the hotel while visiting the only place in this town that actually has good internet?"

Earl didn't comment. He'd noticed that about himself too. Of recent he tended to either forget stuff he needed for work, or, when he did remember everything, he'd then forget to apply the right procedures to get the necessary results—like how he'd forgotten to set the audio recorders to 'voice activated' mode last night.

Almost as if there's something in this weird town that doesn't want us finding out what's happening here. But I've a surefire fix for that, town. From now on, I'll simply write down what I don't wanna forget.

But Earl now put all that out of his mind. With what he'd accidentally discovered this afternoon, it would be hard for Jerome to hide its secrets from him from now on. *Ha ha ha! I'm onto you now, guys! Try and stop me if you can!*

Earl hadn't mentioned his strange discovery to either Keith or Minnie. This was simply him being cautious. He wanted to be certain, absolutely certain of his discovery before letting the others in on it. This was simply the way he operated. As much as possible, Earl tried to figure out most of the variables associated with each project before getting his two associates involved. That way there was less chance of their being derailed into nonproductive blind alleys.

***

What had happened was that shortly after Minnie had left to go lie down in she and Keith's room, Earl's attention had been caught by a bird that had flown past the window. This was in itself nothing peculiar, but while trying to make out what sort of bird it was, Earl had stepped outside onto the balcony for a moment to study the bird in detail. It had been a raven or a crow, large and black and at that moment alighting from the sky.

And it was then, that to his utter surprise, on looking down, he had noticed the raven fly through a young man who was standing down in the parking lot and waving to a woman who was walking towards him.

Forgotten, the bird had meanwhile settled down on one of the shrubs outside the parking lot, and was looking around.

But the discovery had been made. That young man down below, and apparently his girlfriend too, were both ghosts. They seemed solid enough, but they apparently didn't exist on this human plane. On making this discovery, Earl had felt both thrills of fear and also elation. It had been all he could do not to shout out 'Eureka' like that old Greek guy had done all those centuries ago.

There had of course been one other major consideration. This was that it was the bird that was a ghost and not the people. After all, from the evidence so far, Earl had no proof that the it was the humans that had been porous and not the bird. So, while making conversation with Keith through the balcony door as best he could, he kept up his surveillance of the young couple in question, who were still standing down in the parking lot of the Jerome Grand Hotel.

At first it looked as if nothing would happen. The crow or raven that had sparked Earl's discovery had meanwhile flown away again, zipping over an arriving tour bus as it ascended into the sky. That might have been proof enough that the bird was solid, as the tour bus definitely was, and the crow hadn't attempted to fly through the vehicle, but Earl wanted something more definite than that.

And then it happened. Just like that, the young couple faded from view. All of a sudden there was no one down there in the parking lot.

But it wasn't over yet. Earl was still holding his breath from what he'd seen when the same young couple appeared a short distance away. As if they'd merely been hidden by a screen for a few seconds, the pair were still walking along, headed towards the hotel entrance.

Earl was now completely entranced by what was happening down below. He also felt fear, fear that stemmed from the understanding that maybe he was witnessing something he shouldn't be seeing. He'd been researching paranormal phenomena for years now, and yet never before had he stumbled on something quite like this.

If only I could film this! But he knew that he couldn't. All he could do was continue watching.

All this while Keith was still suggesting ways that they could film the ghost in Room 32. Earl was no longer listening; his brother's raised voice came through the balcony door and blew past his ears like storm winds past a bunker. It was a familiar noise he could easily tune out.

Downstairs, however, Earl was about to make a new discovery. The phantom couple had stopped and were chatting with a young woman. An additional layer of strangeness was now added by the fact that their friend was dressed in nineteenth century attire. This wasn't in itself unusual, because the town of Jerome had several period reconstruction set pieces for tourists, and some of the town residents were actors who earned their living by acting the part of old-time characters in these buildings. The reconstructed brothel was a particularly successful version of this.

Seeing as the young woman in question here was carrying on a conversation with two ghosts, Earl quickly realized that she could only be one herself. Either that, or she was a psychic, a medium. But Earl cancelled out the latter option, because once their conversation ended, the young man's girlfriend leaned forward and hugged the women wearing older clothes.

They separated then, with the older ghost turning to walk off in the direction of the town. The woman didn't follow the winding road, however, but instead just stepped off of the parking lot into the countryside and descended the hillside that way, her yellow-and-red dress bobbing up and down with her motion.

Earl had suddenly had a good idea of exactly where it was that the ghost was headed. He'd smiled, understanding that he'd just seen the ghost of one of Jerome's dead prostitutes, who was apparently on her way back home to what in her time had been called the 'Crib District.'

So that was Earl's great discovery; that this town really did shelter two different sorts of people, the living and the dead.

The problem now was how to separate the two kinds of creatures; how to tell them apart. This was a genuine problem, because as far as Earl could tell, in some cases, the ghosts were as solid as the living.

This town supposedly has a population of about four hundred residents, Earl though. *But I suspect the ghosts might just form an additional four hundred. And most likely, these extra folks simply get mistaken for tourists most of the time. Or else, the living townsfolks simply can't see them.*

Down below, the young ghost couple had just climbed onto the just-arrived tour bus. Earl had no idea what to make of that. He however now realized that he was sitting on the verge of possibly the biggest paranormal breakthrough in history.

All he needed to do was figure out how to capture it for others to view also.

"Hey, are you even listening to me?" Keith was asking.

"Huh?" Earl had replied, and had stepped away from the balcony railing. Keith was now standing in the balcony doorway, looking at him curiously.

"What did you say, bro?" Earl had quickly asked.

"I think that to film these ghosts, we need vintage equipment," Keith had replied. "You know, old-school stuff that ain't affected by the hotel's aura, like digital gear clearly is."

Earl had nodded. "Oh, you mean like Polaroid cameras and things like that?"

Keith had nodded and walked over to join Earl by the balcony railing. Despite being the younger of the siblings, he was three inches taller than his elder brother, something that intermittently both bothered and amused Earl.

"What's the matter, dude?" Keith had asked with concern on his face. For his part he'd paid no attention to the parking lot. Keith had just stretched and stared out at the view of town and the countryside.

"Nothing, nothing's wrong," Earl had replied, trying to maintain an aura of neutrality.

"You could have fooled me." Keith had rubbed his cleanshaven chin, pulled his cellphone out of his pants pocket to check the time and then nodded. "Today has an odd vibe to it for sure," he'd told Earl. "First, it's Minnie who's acting weird and now you."

"I'm *not* acting weird," Earl had retorted with more feeling that was usual for him. "I'm just thinking a lot about this problem. You know, we'll soon be leaving here, and so far, we've not recorded anything we can use for our YouTube show."

"Don't sweat it," Keith had replied. "I dunno why, but I got a strong feeling that something big is about to blow up around us. And we'll be right in the middle when it does."

"And hopefully, we'll have the means to record it for the world," Earl had said. "I really hope this retro-tech idea of yours works."

CHAPTER 6

While escorting Nancy downstairs to dinner, Herman pondered how best to broach the subject of the pair of them properly renewing their relationship. Where he was concerned Nancy Lee, comedienne extraordinaire and twice voted 'Funniest Woman in Arizona,' was 'the one that got away,' this being a mistake Herman didn't intend repeating.

Really, I should never have married Louise. In fact, I never would have married her if Nancy hadn't broken up with me. But Nancy left me high and dry back then, and Louise was there for me when I needed a shoulder to cry on; and then of course, one thing led to another and I suppose I let my feelings of gratitude to her for helping through that bad patch in my life cloud my judgement.

Okay, Herman realized that he was being slightly unfair to his ex, the two of them had had some great times (and produced three kids) before things had inexplicably soured between them and pointed them towards the divorce courts. But the facts of the case could never be denied. In this current situation, Herman couldn't help looking unfavorably at Louise. Once the point of comparison was Nancy Lee, Louise could only come in second best.

But how do I tell Nancy of my feelings? I don't wanna rush things, and yet, I can sense she's just waiting for me to propose to her in some way. Not to get married, of course. At least not yet, though that's what I ultimately have in mind too. But she's gonna want me to make some kind of a commitment. Dammit, no one would expect getting a girlfriend later on in life to be more difficult than getting one when you're in your twenties.

Such were Herman Broderick's thoughts, when all of a sudden, he felt a cold breeze blow past him. They were nearing the stairwell, but yet the sudden passage of that chilling current felt so unnatural to

31

Herman that he froze, jerked around, and stared back down the corridor. But just as he expected, there was no one else in sight. He and Nancy were alone in the corridor.

Herman felt goosebumps form on his arms.

He realized that Nancy had felt the same wind that he had; so, he hadn't imagined it. The corridor was suddenly as cold as a freezer and they were both shivering.

"That breeze felt like I imagine a ghost might—cold as ice and in a hurry to get nowhere," she said. "But . . . what I don't get is, where could the breeze possibly have come from? This corridor has no windows and all of the doors are shut."

She was looking at Herman with a worried expression on her face. He was still thinking of something reassuring to tell her, when she gave a start. "Hey, listen, can you hear that?"

Herman at first didn't understand what she meant, but then he heard it too: the soft but rapid patter of feet; the noise of a child's running feet. What was odd about this was that the sound was coming from directly ahead of them, where there was no one in sight. The corridor was brightly lit with no nooks for a child to hid himself or herself. And besides, not only was there no child in the corridor, but as far as Herman knew, from overhearing one of the waiters replying to another guest, there were currently no children registered as guests in the Jerome Hotel.

The unseen feet suddenly seemed to stop running; their noise faded away.

His puzzlement clear on his face he stared at Nancy, who gripped his arm tightly. "Let's get the hell downstairs," she said in a scared voice. "This place is starting to give me the creeps."

"Yes, let's," Herman quickly agreed. "Or else I might start seeing spooks coming through the walls."

No sooner had he said this however, than the sound of running footsteps resumed. This time however, the footsteps were above them, clearly coming from the fourth floor of the building.

If previously the unseen child had been racing away from them, now he or she was headed back towards them, the child's pattering footfalls becoming louder by the instant until finally they ran over the heads of the perplexed pair.

Herman and Nancy instinctively turned around to follow the sound of the child's footsteps, which ceased almost immediately. By now, Nancy was gripping Herman's arm tightly, though neither of them could have said exactly when she'd grabbed such a firm hold of him. On Herman's part, he was trying hard to rationalize what they'd just been hearing. He stared up at the ceiling and thought hard on the puzzle:

Must be the sound of someone's TV—one which actually works in here. . . . This building must have weird acoustics.

Surely that was the problem here. Some freak transmission of sound from one part of the building to another. As a realtor, Herman had experienced similar odd acoustic phenomena in a number of the buildings he'd either rented out or put up for sale.

But even while telling himself this, he felt that he was deceiving himself. This town had a reputation for ghosts. What if those footsteps they'd been hearing . . . ?

No, that's ridiculous. There's no such things as ghosts. I need to keep my mind on the straight and narrow.

He realized that Nancy too was staring up at the ceiling. He realized why she was doing so. Just like himself, she was waiting for the sound of the kid's footsteps to start again, as the child ran back towards them.

So, they both stood there, seemingly not breathing; waiting. But nothing happened; real or imagined, the unseen little boy or little girl had either tired of their fun or been scolded by an adult.

Herman looked down again. Nancy was looking at him. "Ugh, let's just get out of here," he said.

"Yeah," she quickly agreed.

They'd been looking at each other, not at the stairs, and now that they turned to take the last few steps towards the stairwell, they were forced to halt again. This time however, it wasn't a ghost, but a woman was ascending the stairs, a nurse by the looks of her white uniform, which was complete with the folded and pinned nurse's cap.

The nurse, an attractive blonde in maybe her early thirties, nodded curtly to both Herman and Nancy, and then without pause, headed upstairs to the fourth floor.

Herman watched her go with a sudden sense of misgiving. "I think someone may be ill up there," he whispered to Nancy, as the woman's white-stockinged legs vanished up the stairs.

"Or maybe she's the visible mother of that invisible brat," Nancy replied in a nervous voice. "Come on, Herman, let's just get downstairs to the bar. I need a few drinks in me now before we have dinner."

"Me too," Herman agreed.

***

The bar of the Jerome General Hotel was sparsely occupied. There were just two couples seated in booths and five people sitting at the bar proper. When Herman and Nancy entered the room, the bartender was placing a daiquiri in front of a white-haired old gent dressed in clothes better suited to fifty years ago.

Just as with the rest of the interior of the Jerome General Hotel, the bar had been restored to look like it had in days gone by. Each time Herman entered it, he felt like he was stepping into the past, reclaiming part of a world long vanished. Actually, Herman got that feeling from the entire building, as during its renovation, much care had been taken to keep as much of its finished look and furnishing as true to the original as possible.

So now, he guided Nancy to a seat up opposite the bartender, realizing as he did so, that this was how the gentlemen patrons of those bygone days would have guided their ladyfolk to a similar bar a hundred years ago. Once more he got that sense of reentering a lost world.

He wasn't naturally sentimental, but something about this building (or maybe it was this entire town) tugged to his heartstrings in this inexplicable way.

"Two double brandies, please," Nancy was already ordering from the bartender, a stocky, taciturn man named Riley. Herman had already noticed that Riley rarely said much more than the "Good evening," he greeted him with now. Yesterday, he'd tried to engage Riley in conversation about their non-functioning televisions.

"Signal comes and goes, sir," Riley had politely replied, and then, before Herman could ask another question, had turned to pour wine into someone else's glass.

Now, as Riley placed a brandy each before himself and Nancy, Herman considered asking him about the child they had heard running upstairs, but then he thought better of it. Riley had a look in his eye this evening that discouraged questions. And besides, Herman had no idea how he could phrase such a question without sounding silly.

Nancy had already gulped down half of her drink, and he followed suit. He felt better immediately. He didn't want to admit it to himself, but he'd felt something unnerving about that nurse they'd met at the stairway too. He wasn't about to go so far as to suggest that she'd appeared out of nowhere (he knew that was nonsense), but there had been something 'nasty' in the smile she'd thrown at Nancy and himself.

It was almost as if she was on her way upstairs to hurt someone, not to heal them.

He shook away the ridiculous mental assertion. He finished his drink and tried to catch Riley's eye. The bartender finally noticed him and walked over.

"A refill, sir?"

Herman nodded.

"And one for me too," Nancy added, pushing her own emptied glass forward at Riley. "But no more brandy. Give me something sweet—some of that red wine over there."

Riley nodded and turned away again.

"So, what would you like to do after dinner?" Herman asked Nancy. The bar connected directly to the restaurant and, looking through the door that led to it, he could see a waiter serving a plump woman in a green dress in there.

Nancy looked that way too, patted her hair down, and then shrugged. "Oh, I dunno. What do you have in mind?"

Herman thought a bit. His mind hadn't really been on dinner anyway. What he really wanted to get Nancy somewhere private where they could have an intimate conversation.

Okay, so yes, he'd been in her hotel room a lot since their arrival here yesterday. (Wow, was it really such a short time ago, that they'd checked in here? Somehow it seemed much longer.) So, yes, Herman had been in Nancy's room a lot, but her room simply didn't strike him as the right place to discuss their relationship. It lacked a touch of the romantic; if that was the right expression. He wanted to discuss their future in a fittingly emotional setting, a place that they could then both remember fondly when reminiscing in future.

Riley was still busy fetching Nancy's wine, while she herself was staring at Herman expectantly, waiting to hear what he had planned for their evening.

He laughed. "Well, this town doesn't have a movie theater, and we're about to step into arguably their best restaurant anyway."

Nancy laughed. "Yeah, I know. Even a Netflix date is out because of the nonexistent Wi-Fi."

Herman had been about suggesting that he and Nancy simply take a walk through the surrounding countryside after dinner. Up in the hills would be a nice place to have their long-delayed heart-to-heart. But suddenly he felt impelled to comment on the Wi-Fi, the bad cell service and nonexistent TV, a state of affairs unbelievable in modern times. He wanted Riley to hear him, and to pass on his complaints to management. The bartender was approaching them now, bearing their drinks, which he slid before them just as Herman began his angry complaint:

"It's totally unacceptable in modern times for a hotel of this standing not to have working telephones," he said loudly. "I can't call my office, my goddamn cellphone doesn't work, I can't watch television, can't use the internet, can't . . ." he sighed. "Had I known things would be like this here, I never have booked this place."

While speaking, Herman had been careful to avoided looking directly at Riley; he didn't wish to appear too confrontational. But since Riley was standing directly in front of Nancy, he couldn't look at her either. Which had left him with just two options: he could have turned around and spoken out into the room, which, although it would have perfectly fit in with the impression of general disgust he desired to create, would have required an awkward rotation on his bar stool.

But, not wishing to go to the trouble of doing that, Herman had instead simply turned left, which had meant that while speaking, he was staring at the trio of young persons, two men and a woman, who were seated on that side of the bar. There was a vacant stool between he and the nearest of the trio, a plumpish bearded man in faded denim, but his voice had been sufficiently loud to have been misinterpreted by the trio as being addressed to them in particular and maybe the room in general.

Herman almost sighed when the bearded man nodded back at him. "Yah, I feel your pain, sir," was his clearly amused reply. "And so, please permit me to venture an illogical reply to your question."

Herman nodded. The man's intrusion meant he didn't have to look at the taciturn Riley yet. He now recognized the young trio as also rooming up on the third floor, in two facing rooms at the far end of the corridor.

"Well," the bearded man went on, "I'll try to make this as simple and painless as I can." He paused as if for effect and then added: "Sir, the general lack of telecoms in this hotel is caused by the ghosts in the building."

This explanation was so unexpected that it was all Herman could do not to laugh out loud. The man however seemed serious. Herman wondered if he was drunk, but his voice was stable, and he was only drinking a coke. His general manner also didn't seem to be that of someone on narcotics. That of course, left just one other option: that this fat man in the denim getup was crazy.

The man was shaking his head. "Sir, the whole town's got bad reception. There's claims it's the residual copper in the hills messing up the signals, but I ain't buyin' that explanation."

"Sorry, but who are you? And why are you so sure of this?" Herman asked him. His initial thought had been to discourage the man with a brusque reply and then turn back to Nancy, but then he remembered the odd phenomenon he and she had both recently experienced—those inexplicable footsteps in the corridor. He figured there was no harm in hearing more of the man's rants.

"Yeah, I'd better introduce myself," the man said. "I'm Earl Roche, paranormal researcher, founder, along with my brother Keith here, of the Paranormal Research Brothers organization. You might have heard of us—we're big on the internet as one of the most reliable evaluators of ghostly activity you'll find anywhere on the planet."

Herman shook his head. "I'm not really into the spook scene."

Earl airily waved the comment aside. "The lovely young lady with us is Minnie Connors, anchorwoman extraordinaire."

"Hi there!" Both Earl's brother Keith and Minnie waved to Herman, who waved back.

"Hi, Earl," Nancy next greeted from behind Herman.

That made Herman turn to stare at her. (Riley was now down at the far end of the bar, washing a set of glasses.) "You know him from somewhere?"

"Oh, I met Mrs. Lee here at this same bar yesterday," Earl explained.

"Oh, call me Nancy," Nancy said. "Earl, I already told ya that."

"Yeah, and my name's Herman," Herman said, turning back towards Earl. He gestured past Earl, at the man's two companions. "So, are you three ghosthunters then?"

Minnie nodded back. "Only, for a town that's reputedly a ghost colony, we've been having very little luck with finding them here in Jerome," she said.

Keith nodding his agreement. "Yeah, it's almost like they're all hiding from us."

Herman felt he had to comment on this. "I don't wanna be a party-pooper, but couldn't it just be that there's no ghosts here at all?"

Earl laughed smugly, like a man possessing secret knowledge. Herman realized that he liked the man. Earl had something studious about him; aside from this crazy obsession of his, he had a day job for sure, and a responsible one at that. His brother on the other hand had a slacker vibe to him, while he couldn't place their lady friend; temperament-wise, she seemed a mixture of both men.

"And so, I take it you really believe what you just said, I mean about the spooks—alright, ghosts if you guys prefer—being the ones responsible for screwing up digital devices here in Jerome?" After saying this, Herman laughed in an attempt to make the question appear silly.

Earl Roche however didn't laugh. He simply shrugged. "Well, you gotta admit it's the explanation that makes the best sense." Then, rather than saying more on the topic, he gestured into the room, to an empty booth in the corner near the restaurant door. "Hey, since we all know each other now, why don't we move over there? Sitting at a table we can all see and hear each other better."

Herman looked over at the booth. "That makes sense, but Nancy and I were just having a few drinks before having dinner," he explained. "I don't think—"

"I've just about lost any appetite for food," Nancy interrupted him with a laugh. "Let's go sit at the table over there. I wanna hear what the kid has to say about this."

Herman sighed, as it looked like his plans to monopolize Nancy for the evening had just been torpedoed. Then he nodded to Earl and his companions. "Okay, let's head over there."

After ordering fresh rounds of drinks, everyone carried what remained of their current beverages and relocated to the corner booth. Herman and Nancy sat on one side of the table and the three ghosthunters on the other.

"Everyone in the ghost hunting scene calls us the Paranormal Brothers,' Earl laughed once everyone was seated. "But enough of that, I'll get straight to the point—don't wanna delay your dinners."

Earl and Nancy nodded, and then Nancy asked: "So what's this about ghostly activity affecting all the phones, our TVs, and the internet?"

"Not *all* phones," Keith answered before Earl could. "I'm sure you've both heard television noise coming from some other rooms on our floor. The spook activity is specific, confined to particular rooms. To make his point, he gestured to the opposite end of the bar room, where a woman with a cellphone held to her ear was making angry retorts into it.

"Sometimes it shifts tho'," Minne added. "Like the ghosts get bored with causing mischief in just one place and seek someone else to pester." She sipped some wine and laughed. "Or maybe, they've a quota of scares to make each month, and you get relief once that's filled up."

"Hey, that was supposed to be my line," Nancy said with a laugh. After looking at Herman, she nodded back at the girl. "Yeah, we noticed that; there's at least three rooms on our floor that seem to have good television reception, and I've definitely heard a phone conversation being carried on in the room right near the stairs." Then her brow creased up in puzzlement. "But what causes it?"

"Please, please don't tell me it's just ghosts," Herman objected because he felt he needed to. *Or else we'll soon be discussing little men from Planet X, and how they plan on taking over the Earth, starting here in no-importance-at-all Jerome, AZ.*

Earl took up the explanation. "Well, sorry to disappoint you there, Herman, but the ghost explanation in the only one that fits the facts."

"Which are?" Herman asked.

"I'd better spare you the technical details, or else we'll be here all night long," Earl replied. "But suffice it to say that none of the other explanations—bad network signals for instance, or irradiated copper deposits with suspicions of uranium ore somewhere nearby—hold water once properly examined."

"The easiest test for that is to compare the situation here in Jerome to that in the neighboring communities of Cottonwood and Clarkdale," Keith added. "Both of those places are completely normal as regards to telecoms."

"And both also lack this town's large complement of supernatural residents," Minnie added.

They paused as Riley set a tray of drinks before them.

"Hey, what's your take on paranormal activity messing up this town's telecoms?" Herman asked the bartender.

For a moment it looked as if Riley wouldn't reply, but then he smiled slightly and said, "Left to me, sir, I'd say that it's both entirely likely and unlikely that that's the case here. But if you don't mind my sayin' so, I'm sure dead folks have better things to do in the afterlife that play switchboard operator."

That stated, he served everyone their drinks, collected their used glasses and the empty bottles and departed again for the bar.

"Ugh, that guy is super-creepy. He almost scares me more than the dead do," Minnie said with a mock shudder, once Riley was out of earshot.

"He certainly is a character," Herman agreed.

"That reply of his was the mother of noncommittal," Nancy said. " 'Entirely likely and unlikely?' What the hell is that supposed to mean?"

Earl laughed. "That's our Riley for y'all." This time around he'd ordered a glass of beer, which he now raised to his lips and took a sip from. When he put it down again, he had an amusing white froth on his upper lip that looked like a second mustache.

Herman sipped his whiskey. He found Earl's assertion both corny and creepy. Corny, because the man had skipped giving any facts to back up his assertions; creepy, because, looking past Nancy, he could see the woman who was making a phone call. She was still speaking, though now she looked less angry than earlier. On an instinct he felt his pockets for his own cellphone, but then remembered he'd left it upstairs in his room. What point was there in lugging the cell around if he wasn't likely to get any network signal?

And yet, I've not yet tried the hills. Maybe up near the mines I'll be able to get a call out to someone.

"What I would like to know," Nancy was telling Earl, "is, how *she* can make a phone call, but I can't? Maybe she uses a different cellular provider, or... maybe...do some of these ghosts attach themselves to specific people and haunt just those people?"

Herman grinned at the carrier comment Nancy made. She surely was spot on there and surly added the ghost remark to keep Earl and party entertained.

"I dunno." Earl replied, seeming to reply to Nancy's latter part of observation. "Sometimes it seems like it. I'm still researching how it works."

"Kid, what do ya know?" Nancy asked with quite a bit of frustration.

Earl shrugged. "Well, this building reputedly has lots poltergeist activity. I don't know if you've yet experienced the self-opening-and-closing doors?"

Nancy gave a little shudder and shook her head. "Thank God I haven't."

"Don't be so grateful yet," Minnie said. "The hotel poltergeists are certain to visit you in a short while. You guys just arrived here. They seem to like to allow people to settle in properly first before they start banging the doors and moving stuff around."

Herman gave Earl an alarmed look. "Does this really happen . . . on a regular basis?"

He nodded. "Depends on the guests. Some people seem to provide a focus for paranormal activity: they attract more attention than others. I, for instance, don't get much in the way of poltergeists, while Minnie here . . ."

Herman and Nancy both looked at Minnie.

"It's only happened twice, but both times were as creepy as fuck," Minnie said.

"So . . . what happened?" Nancy asked.

Minnie first looked around the room as if scared that some ghosts were listening to her, and then she replied: "Well, the first time, I was eating a sandwich and it moved. One moment it was right in front of me and the next moment it was at the far end of the coffee table. I was so surprised that I didn't understand what had happened. I'd been reaching for the sandwich and suddenly it was nowhere in sight. I thought I'd dropped it on the floor and bent to look for it, but it wasn't down on the rug. I finally located my sandwich beside the flower vase." She stared challengingly at the others. "Explain that away if you can."

"I can't," Herman truthfully admitted. "What happened the second time?"

"That one happened in the bathroom," Keith said, smiling at Nancy. "Minnie was in there, doing whatever it is you ladies do that takes an hour and a half before you go shopping."

"We do it because you expect us to," Nancy replied with an easy laugh. "If no one paid any attention to the amount of time women spent in the bathroom, we'd soon tire of remaining in there. So, what happened to Minnie in the bathroom?"

"The toilet flushed itself," Minnie said, with a shudder. "Thankfully, I wasn't sitting on it at the time or I'd have screamed the house down."

"For a ghosthunter, you seem remarkably easy to frighten," Herman said, but then instantly regretted saying so when Nancy elbowed him and said, "Hey, let the girl finish her story."

Herman nodded to Minnie. "Sorry, please go on."

There was silence at their table then, and Minnie finished her story: "Well, I was soaking in the bathtub, almost falling asleep, when I saw it happen. Our bathroom has one of those old-style faucets—the type you manually turn—and I saw it moving downward. At first, I thought it might just be a mechanical plumbing fault, like maybe the water cabinet was too full or something like that, but the lever kept going down just like it had a hand been pressing on it. It depressed all the way to the point where the toilet flushed, then it flipped back up again." Her eyes had grown large and she shivered with the memory. "That alone would've been creepy enough, but at the same time as the flusher handle depressed like that, a cold wind was suddenly blowing in the bathroom." She looked at Keith.

Keith nodded and continued her story: "That's the really weird part of this. The cold wind was first blowing through our hotel room. It wasn't fierce or anything like that, but I got the clear impression of something unnatural being in there with me. Then the cold feeling disappeared for a few seconds and I heard the toilet flush. And then Minnie suddenly emerged from the bathroom looking pale as a sheet and dripping bubbles like she'd leapt out of the tub and run for her life. She ran at me and grabbed me tight, and the next thing that we both felt . . ."

". . . The cold wind blew past us both and seemed to be heading for the front door," Minnie finished. "Then it was gone for good."

While speaking she'd slipped her hand over Keith's and was gripping it tightly, so that Herman quickly deduced the pair were a couple.

"That *is* scary," Nancy said. "You mean that really happened to you two?"

Minnie and Keith both nodded. "Yeah, as surely as daylight is daylight and we're both sitting here now."

"But of course, we didn't catch it on film," Earl said glumly, staring at the remains of his beer. "That, people, is the current bane of my existence."

"Yeah, that is the problem now," Keith agreed. "Earl's vacation will be over by the end of the week and yet, we're finding it impossible to capture anything on film."

Herman wasn't really interested in whether or not Earl was able to capture his spooks on camera. He was concerned about something else. "Tell me," he asked Earl, "these ghosts of yours—are they dangerous?"

44

Earl smiled and shook his head. "Supposedly not. At least, I've so far not read any accounts of those here in the Jerome Grand Hotel actually harming anyone. But then, maybe I've not read widely enough. There's stories all over the internet about the spirits that supposedly haunt this place, for instance, there's an old miner guy, a kid, a guy who supposedly fell off his balcony, a nurse or two, along with one or two others; and then there's all sorts of—"

"Hey, back up a bit," Herman said. "Did you say *nursing* ghosts?" He felt chilled as he remembered the woman they'd seen ascending the stairs.

"Yes, why would there be nursing ghosts in this place?" Nancy asked.

It was Keith who replied her question. "About a hundred years ago, this building place used to be a hospital. That was around the time when there was a horrible flu epidemic in the region that killed lots of people. Legend has it that the ghosts of some of those who died here never left." He frowned. "Maybe they're the poltergeists?"

"That strikes me as very funny," Nancy said. "Imagine a ghost running into the bathroom to take an invisible crap."

Herman would have asked for more detail about the ghosts, but Minnie said, "You know, I think our bartender Riley knows a hell of a lot more about the spirits haunting this building than he's letting on."

"Yeah, I agree," Keith nodded, then stared at Nancy and Herman while jerking his thumb towards the bar. "It's almost like he's scared to talk about what he knows." Keith scratched his chin. "I wonder why that is though."

Nancy burst out laughing. "Maybe he doesn't want the poltergeists all leaving the hallways and taking up residence in his rooms. And speaking of Riley, let's all have another round of drinks, on me this time."

This comment of hers caused loud affirmation from the three ghosthunters.

Herman hid his exasperation at this further unexpected turn of events. Nancy Lee wasn't an alcoholic, but during all those years touring she'd clearly become quite the social drinker and party animal. She could hold her liquor with the best of them, and seeing as their three younger companions also seemed in the mood to get a little drunk, there would clearly be no romantic discourse about he and Nancy's shared future tonight.

Aw shucks, he thought as Riley stepped away from his bar to take their orders, *Let's just drink away the evening. Hopefully, once everyone's had a few more brews, they'll feel the need for some food as well. Have to be quickly though, before the restaurant closes. I don't recall seeing any pizza joints nearby.*

Herman thought on what the ghosthunters had said. He still thought the trio were leading him on. He'd so far not experienced any poltergeist activity . . . Okay, there had been those inexplicable footsteps in the corridor that were indirectly responsible for this meeting with the three. So yes, that might count. But . . . had that nurse actually been a specter?

I really doubt that, Herman thought grimly. *That woman was as solid as I am.*

The drinks arrived then, and from that point on it seemed to Herman a good idea to forget about ghosts for the time being.

CHAPTER 7

The next morning, Earl suggested to his companions that they make an impromptu trip into town.

"Forget it," Minnie whispered, and then she rolled over on her belly, pulled the bedcovers over her head, and went back to sleep.

It was left to Earl to rouse his brother and get him into the bathroom to clean himself up.

***

Last night had been . . . actually Earl no longer remembered too much about what happened after he, Keith and Minnie had begun drinking with the older couple from Black Canyon. What he did remember was a pleasant alcoholic fog filled with laughter (Nancy Lee was, after all, one of Arizona's foremost comedians). Somewhere amidst all that they may have had dinner. Or maybe they hadn't; it really hadn't seemed to matter.

As to how and why Earl had awoken on the floor of Keith and Minnie's hotel room and not in his own very comfortable hotel bed, Earl believed he remembered that quite well.

They—meaning his ghost-hunting team and their two new and equally inebriated older friends—had staggered up the stairs together at about 1 a.m. in the morning; and then after waving Herman and Nancy away along the corridor, Earl, Keith and Minnie had returned to their own two rooms to discover that they no longer remembered which room was which. Was Earl's room the one on their left, or was that Keith's and Minnie's? In the end they'd drunkenly figured it didn't matter either way, had pushed open the first door Minnie had successfully gotten open and had all staggered in there. Earl had curled up on the floor and fallen asleep almost before he'd gotten himself properly laid down.

After which . . . he'd woken up this morning.

***

Once he was fully awake, Earl had felt an immediate sense of purpose. All he saw before him for a moment was the image of yesterday's ghostly prostitute, walking straight downhill, surely heading towards what used to be called Husband's Alley.

And wherever she has gone to, I intend to follow, he told himself as he waited for Keith to emerge from the bathroom. Minnie was now completely buried in covers, with a sky-blue pillow pulled over her head to drown out all intrusive conversation.

"C'mon, bro, what are we going to do down there anyway? I've got a hangover like . . ." Keith looked at the wall clock. "Hey, it's just ten in the morning. You got a date with a hot chick or what?"

"Just get dressed, while I go change too," Earl said, though he had a hangover too. "If I was meeting a lady, I wouldn't want you along, would I?"

He waited long enough to ensure that Keith didn't climb back into bed and snuggle up to Minnie, then hurried over to his own suite to tidy himself up a bit.

About fifteen minutes later, the Roche brothers descended to the lobby of the Jerome Grand Hotel, and then descended the long front stairway outside the hotel that led down to the parking lot, and then finally, set off on foot for the town below.

"Why aren't we taking the van?" Keith asked.

"I feel too hungover to drive safely anywhere." Then he wagged a finger in his brother's face. "Uh uh, bro, don't even suggest it. You look exactly how I feel, so no. And besides, I don't remember where I left the van keys."

"We should wait for one of the tour buses then," Keith griped as they walked briskly downhill. "What can possibly be so urgent this morning?"

"Just come on. I gotta check something out, and I need your impressions on it too," Earl insisted.

CHAPTER 8

Nowadays Jerome, Arizona, no longer had a red-light district. Such a district had however existed (and flourished) back in the old 'boomtown' days, when the copper mines were running twenty-four hour shifts and copper ore was being carved out of the mountain by the ton. Back then in the late nineteenth and early twentieth centuries, Jerome boasted of almost twenty brothels, almost as many saloons and a measly four churches, meaning it was no surprise the place got dubbed "The Wickedest City in the West," on account of the amount of whoring, gambling, drug using (mostly opium), and the sheer amount of murders that happened there.

Back in those bygone days, when Jerome had been chock-full of brothels and prostitutes, one could find those houses of pleasure just about anywhere in the town, with a good portion of that red-light behavior occurring on its main street.

But once the citizens decided to act a little more civilized, all of those 'dens of sin' were moved off of Main Street to where was back then called the Crib District, where the town's 'soiled angels' could continue plying their trade of entertaining lonely and lusty men.

All of that legendary bad behavior was long in the town's past now. Nowadays, Main Street was just that; Jerome's main drag, which housed mainly business establishments catering to tourists and artists, the latter of which Jerome had a flourishing, if small, community.

Keith and Earl made their way to Main Street. Keith was still bemused by how Earl had hustled him out of bed; and he was trying to make it alive through the hangover he'd brought along from the night before.

Last night had been a strange one alright. All that drinking they'd done . . . and now not really remembering anything else. His mind was a blank, almost like a slate wiped clean. He remembered who he was and all that, but somehow, he'd forgotten most of yesterday's conversations with Herman and Nancy.

He shrugged as another throb of headaches swept through his skull like a herd of stampeding horses flattening everything in their path.

**

Keith Roche had never really believed in ghosts. He wasn't sure he believed in them now. Having faith in the spirits of the departed dead had never sat well with him. Trying to locate and talk to the dead seemed almost like joining some kind of religion, and hell no, Keith wasn't even the slightest bit religious.

So why do I do it then? he pondered as he followed Earl further and further along Main Street while the sun rose higher in the sky and threatened a very hot day.

But really, he knew why he hunted ghosts alongside his brother. Doing so gave him the chance to confirm that there really was something 'out there'; maybe a higher power, maybe an afterlife. Something, anyway.

And Keith was very dedicated to Earl's ghost-hunting vision. He knew their Paranormal Research Brothers organization, was what kept Earl sane amidst the financial rat race. Earl was pulling his steady nine-to-five, almost burying himself with work and would soon make senior manager at the bank. But Keith knew his brother had no love whatsoever for the job he did; to him it was simply a means to a regular paycheck that let him afford the things he really enjoyed in life.

Keith really admired that; he'd tried holding down a nine-to-five more than once, but it simply hadn't worked for him; either he quit the job or the job quit him.

Outside of his painting—which was a thing he could pick up when he felt the stirrings of inspiration and put down gain anytime he felt like having a beer with friends—Keith lacked discipline. In that sense he was different from Minnie, who had the discipline to hold down a regular job, but lacked sufficient motivation to become a success at anything; which was why, despite her high IQ, all she did was waitressing and supermarket floor work.

Minnie has no drive for success. All she wants is love and babies.

Keith wondered why they were still together. Sure, babies were great, but only if they belonged to other couples. Keith had no time for that family nonsense. Babies, both their ceaseless noise and the ceaseless attention they required, cramped an artist's spirit. It wasn't like one could just make kids and then hand them over to the US government to look after till they turned eighteen. If you made kids, you had to look after them, or else you were irresponsible. Keith thought it was even more irresponsible to make kids you didn't want in the first place.

Keith and Earl Roche walked past restaurants, tour guides servicing those who were paranormally curious (Ghost Town Tours), and a few drinking establishments outside of which Keith stared pleadingly at his brother, his eyes holding the request that they slip inside and have a beer or two to help beat up his hangover; but in each case Earl was firm in his refusal to dissuaded from their still-unknown destination.

Finally, Keith and Earl arrive at the Jerome Avenue junction, at the end of which lay the area of town that had once been its red-light district.

Of course, now there were no brothels in sight, no gaudily painted women of the night offering their bodies for sale, no drunk and rowdy men looking for a roll in the hay, and definitely no 'cribs,' those shacks where those prostitutes who weren't in the employ of a brothel had entertained their clients.

All that greeted them now was concrete road, artisan shops, a confectionary, and the occasional pickup truck rolling past. The two Roche brothers had stopped beside the Mine Museum, while opposite them across the road stood the famous Connor Hotel, the ground floor of which was Jerome's equally famous Spirit Bar, the sight of which reminded Keith of how much he wanted a drink.

Keith sighed when he understood where Earl had brought them too.

"Bro, what in the . . . are we doing here?"

"Here is where we're gonna crack this ghost thing," Earl said.

Keith looked at him like he was crazy. "Here? In broad daylight too? Whoever heard of a ghost walking about in the daytime?"

"You'd be surprised," Earl said. "Let me tell you exactly what I noticed yesterday evening down in the hotel parking lot. I was gonna mention it to you and Minnie after dinner, but then we got sidetracked."

Keith pressed a hand to his temples at the memory of how 'sidetracked' they'd all gotten. "Hey, Earl, don't *you* have a hangover too?"

Earl grimaced and shrugged. "I do, and a real bad one at that. But I can't let it get in my way here." He gestured down Jerome Avenue, where a young woman had just emerged from a shop doorway. "This morning's mission is a ghost stakeout. What you and I are gonna do this morning, is simply keep watch, okay?"

Keith nodded. "Okay, so we'll keep watch. But what's this all about? I still don't get it."

"Okay, let me explain then."

Keith listened as Earl told him about the crow that had flown through a man's body and also about the man's ghost girlfriend and the old-time hooker they'd afterwards been talking to. When Earl was done speaking, Keith gasped. "Dude, for real? That actually happened yesterday?"

Earl slowly nodded. "For real. And that's why we're here now to keep a vigil. That ghost lady must've come down here. I'm certain of it."

"Do you think she might be our grandaunt Nora?"

Earl shook his head. "No. I'm not ever sure now that Nora Brown is our grandaunt. I think gramps was pulling our leg that day. You know how he always liked to tell a tall tale."

Keith thought on that for a while. "Yeah, I guess you're right. Too late to ask the old guy now anyway."

"Besides, that couldn't have been Nora yesterday," Earl said. "That ghost girl was ravingly pretty, and you know how Nora supposedly wasn't anything to look at."

Keith mused on the situation for a little while; oddly enough, thinking was helping his hangover. According to their maternal grandfather, who'd been quite the hell-raiser in his younger days, Nora Brown—once Jerome's most notorious madam—was their great grandaunt. Nora Brown had owned a thriving brothel right along this stretch of street they were observing now.

"Alright, I'm with you on this," Keith said. "But where do we set up? Where do we . . . ?" He suddenly realized a glaring omission in their plan: "Earl, if we're supposed to do ghost surveillance here, why did we walk all that way down from the hotel and leave all of our gear in our rooms? Why didn't we just load everything we need—the EMF readers and other stuff, into the van and drive down here? Okay, yeah, you said you don't remember where the van's key is, but we could have waited till you found it and instead driven down here later in the day, when neither of us would still be hungover. Yeah, yeah, I know what you're gonna say next—none of our gear worked in the hotel—but that don't mean it won't work here."

It seemed crazy to Keith that Earl would overlook such basic logistics. *Wow, my bro really is hungover this morning.*

But Earl smiled. "Cool down. Today is just for surveillance. Before carting a vanload of stuff down here and alarming everyone in sight, we need to first of all make certain that I'm right. Remember, we'd been drinking yesterday afternoon too. So those ghostly folks I saw might have been nothing more than a beer illusion. I'm sure I was clear-headed and clear-eyed when I had that experience, but now I realize that it wouldn't have taken more than a few shifting shadows to fake me into thinking the bird went through the man, and my interpretation of everything else that happened afterwards was built on that shaky foundation." He pointed across the street to the Connor Hotel entrance. "And to answer your first question: We'll each take one side of the street. You browse through those shops there and I'll work through this side."

"What exactly are we looking for?"

"Anything out of the ordinary."

"In this fucking town. Man, be serious."

"I mean people that don't look or act ordinary. My theory is that a good percentage of the people in Jerome are actually ghosts in the flesh."

Keith didn't argue. The whole spinoff investigation was beginning to sound kooky. *But then, I'm here in town with nothing else to do, and for some reason, the more we talk about this the better my head feels, so . . .*

"Let's get started," he told his brother. "But I really need some breakfast in me first."

"Oh . . . alright," Earl grudgingly agreed. "I'm beginning to feel hungry myself." Then, seeing how Keith's gaze had suddenly fixed on the entrance to the Spirit Bar across the street, he wagged a finger in his younger brother's face. "No alcohol whatsoever. We both need clear heads for this."

Keith nodded and pointed down Jerome Avenue. "Let's head down to the English Kitchen then, for a bit of breakfast." The English Kitchen sat right at the end of the street and directly faced a winery that sat in the old red-light district.

But Earl shook his head. "We'll be working our way down there anyway, and I want to be sure that when we get there, we're actually concentrating on looking at the people and not looking at our food." He gestured across the street. "Come on, I recall seeing a diner a short distance after the Connor Hotel."

That agreed on, the brothers headed on down Main Street.

While they ate, Keith decided that, so as not to waste the entire day on what he now viewed as Earl's wild goose chase, he'd drop by the

Jerome Artists Co-Op further up Main Street later on in the day and ask them if they ever exhibited work by hungry, struggling, and unknown out-of-town artists. He was certain that the answer would be negative, but figured it couldn't at all hurt to try.

Once they'd both been fortified with a hearty breakfast and perked up by several cups of coffee, the brothers returned to Jerome Avenue and split up.

And it was then, as Keith crossed over to the right side of the road to begin his arranged surveillance, that the world shifted around him.

Suddenly, right when he should have stepped up onto the sidewalk, daylight became nighttime. The sky overhead was dark and the building he'd been making for looked completely different, in addition to which all of its lights were on.

Keith froze for a second. No, this wasn't happening. Bewildered by the sudden change, he spun around to look at Earl, but Earl was no longer on the opposite sidewalk. Instead, where his elder brother and a young lady listening to music on earphones had previously been the only people on the sidewalk over there by the Connor Hotel entrance, that entire side of the street was now filled with a rowdy crowd of people. The hotel building still stood there, but now it had the name Connor's Corner instead.

Keith's shock had prevented him from realizing that his side of the street was just as fully occupied by rowdy men and women.

In keeping with this general increase in the street's human population, were the number of houses it now had. Buildings, large and small, now lined both sides of the road. All windows were open and light streamed out from these to help disperse the darkness. The disconnected sound of drums, pianos, and trumpets punctuated the human noise.

Still confused, Keith looked up. There was a moon hanging overhead, full and yellow and somehow ominous. He looked down again and his gaze snagged on a nearby house sign: "Butter."

A short distance from this building's front entrance, a drunk middle-aged man was being held upright by an equally drunk woman, whose generous mammary assets were almost spilling out of her tight corset. But no, the prostitute wasn't that drunk: Keith suddenly made out her nimble fingers dipping into the drunk's jacket pocket and returning with his wallet.

He felt too perplexed to shout out an alarm. Not that doing so would have done any good. The lady pickpocket was too expert: once she had the man's bankroll, she quickly propped him up against a wall and lost herself in the crowd. Unaware that he had been robbed, the drunk slid down the wall and lay on the ground. Other carousers walked past him like he wasn't there.

Now the smell of the place hit Keith, a reek of alcohol and unwashed bodies. Keith finally understood. This was the Crib District of Jerome's past. Somehow, while crossing the road he'd been spirited back in time. He was now in the midst of the town's long dead miners and those equally famous dead prostitutes.

A sense of alarm now replaced Keith's wonder. *Oh yes, I'm a man of an artistic temperament, who accompanies his elder brother on his ghost hunting jaunts to boost his artistic inspiration, but even so, I've no desire to become trapped in the past. And, worse still, what if I'm not trapped in the past at all? What if I'm simply hallucinating all this? What if I've finally done too much drinking and it's fractured my fragile psyche!?*

As loud drunken men and flirty, avaricious women jostled him left and right, Keith took stock of his situation. *The smart thing for me to do right now is cross back over to the other side of the road again, and so reverse whatever process brought me here. Yes, that's what I'll do; head back over there, join up with Earl again and pretend this never happened. I won't even mention it to Earl; he might be so thrilled by the idea of seeing the past for himself that he'll insist we come back to it!*

So that's what Keith did. He stepped down off of the sidewalk, which was much less maintained that in his day and age, onto the main road (which was in equally bad shape, its surface being all cracked up) and dashed back across.

He heaved a massive sigh of relief when he reached the other side, but then realized his effort had been for nothing.

Nothing about the world had changed. He was still inexplicably trapped in Jerome's past, in the old red-light district. There was no Connor Hotel here; the building he was standing in front of was still named Connor's Corner. Seemingly the same pile of bricks, but with its previous name.

Dammit, what the hell am I gonna do now? Keith thought, as a sense of panic began setting in. He'd now begun examining himself. To his surprise, he was dressed just like the other men here, in faded old-time clothes and a threadbare hat. Like . . .

Just like I'm a miner myself.

He checked his pockets. He had two dollars and fifty cents. It was old money too, not the modern cash he'd had on leaving the restaurant with his brother just now.

Keith noticed a heavily made-up blonde giving him the eye. She was standing in the doorway of a small shack a few yards away. Just like the lady pickpocket, she was almost spilling out of her dress; she had a whole lot to sell and she wasn't shy about displaying her wares. She smiled at Keith and then suggestively rubbed her hands between her legs. He shook his head and quickly moved on. When, after taking a few paces, he looked back, the blonde woman was entering the shack in the company of two bearded men.

Keith decided that right now, there was just one way to keep himself from losing his mind. That was to have a drink; more than one if possible.

Thanking God (or whoever was responsible for moving him back in time) for at least being considerate enough to leave him with some money, he walked over to the nearest open building entrance and stepped inside. Once through the front door, he made a beeline for the bar.

"Bartender, gimme a double brandy, fast!"

Now that *really* scared Keith, realizing that even his voice had been transformed to the thick uneducated drawl of a turn-of-the-previous-century miner.

CHAPTER 9

"Keith, Earl. Hey, where'd everyone go off to?"

Once she'd confirmed that she was along in the hotel room, Minnie rubbed her eyes and then sat up in bed. She still felt very groggy, but managed to stabilize herself to a degree. Then she gripped her head in her hands and groaned. *Wow, it's totally unlike me to drink so much!*

However, the hangover only threatened her; she felt better than she thought she should after consuming as much alcohol as she had the previous night.

After a while of cradling her head she let go of it and looked around the hotel room. This was when she noticed the note on the nightstand.

'Gone into town with Earl. Not sure when I'll get back. Love you.' it read.

"Love you too," she told the note, then crumpled it up and got out of bed to go and use the bathroom.

Minnie felt a lot better once she had brushed her teeth. Now, she remembered Earl trying to wake her up earlier in the day. She looked in the fridge and found half of a pack of chocolate chip cookies. She ate one of those, and then, before remembering that the TV wouldn't work, picked up the remote control and aimed it at the device.

She was surprised when the TV initially showed a clear picture. But then, as if surprised itself that it was working, it resumed its familiar pattern of wavy static lines and washed-out pictures.

Minnie switched the device off again. *Damn this place*, she thought. *Nothing works except the people. If the phone worked, I could easily call Earl and Keith and find out where the both of them are.*

It was going to be a boring day if she was alone. She decided that if neither man returned to the hotel room in the next hour, she'd leave for town to do some sightseeing of her own. There was that Jerome Artists gallery Keith had been wanting to explore, but which for some reason, he'd never gotten the chance to visit. Or had they? Minnie really wasn't sure. She didn't think the two of them had gone there, but then they just might have.

Since checking in here two weeks ago, my memory keeps playing tricks on me. She looked over at a pile of recording equipment that hadn't found space in Earl's hotel room. *You know, maybe Earl is right about the ghosts messing with our heads to keep us from recording them.*

Last night had been fun though. Minnie thought the sheer amount of drinking they'd done—those liquid valiums she secretly referred to her shots as—sure did have a kick to them. She did remember that Nancy Lee had to be the funniest woman alive. Minnie hadn't laughed that much in ages.

But then suddenly, sadness and apprehension filled her.

I still haven't told Keith that I'm pregnant. Each time I want to, something seems to get in the way. I have to do it soon. I really have to do it soon, before I start getting morning sickness and he works it out for himself. Keeping this to myself is almost driving me crazy with worry.

Minnie had found out she was pregnant three weeks ago. For the first week after that confirmatory trip to the doctor, she'd put off telling Keith about it because she wanted to break the news during their 'vacation' in Jerome. But for some reason, ever since arriving in Jerome, the right (or proper) moment to break the news to Keith had never seemed to come.

Minnie knew that her reluctance to tell her boyfriend he was going to be a daddy came from her knowledge of his aversion to fatherhood. Yes, she knew that once she told Keith she was pregnant, he would instantly protest, insisting he wasn't cut out to be a father and also insist on her having an abortion.

Minnie, however, had no intention of terminating her pregnancy. She was twenty-eight now, very much old enough to be a mother. From matching her mother's age to her own, she knew her mother had been twenty-four when she'd given birth to her. Just like her mother,

Minnie was having this baby and that was that. Keith's oppositions would run off of her like water off of a duck's back.

But why then am I so bothered? Why not wait until he starts noticing?

She knew what the problem was. She wasn't scared of him leaving her if she insisted on having their child. She knew that wouldn't happen. She knew Keith loved her with all of his heart. What she was worried about, was that if she forced Keith to become a daddy, he would then resent his own child. She knew that many fathers who welcomed an unwelcome child to the world soon relented their initial hardline stance, their hearts melted by their son or daughter's innocent cuteness; but there were also those other men who simply transferred their anger towards the mother to the child and didn't even realize they'd done so. That child would grow up knowing at a subconscious level that his father disliked him for some reason, but would be unable to understand why.

It doesn't seem worth it, bringing a child into this already hateful world to be further hated by his own parent. She sighed and felt like crying. But I really want this baby! I'm ready to be a mother now! I want Keith's baby and I want him to want it too! But how can I change his mind so that he realizes his child won't be an impediment to his artistic temper . . . Uh, what was that? What just happened?

Something odd had just occurred around Minnie, but for the moment she didn't know what it was. All that she was aware of, was that something unusual had just taken place in her vicinity. It had happened close to her, and both her peripheral vision and the outskirts of her mind had latched onto it, but the rest of her—mind and body— had been so preoccupied with how to tell Keith about their pregnancy that she'd missed noticing what the unusual happening was.

She froze and waited. She had a sudden sense of not being alone in the hotel room. She also hoped that whatever she'd not noticed wouldn't repeat itself. It had been something quite creepy, of that she was quite certain.

She sat and waited, with each moment stretching out into the metaphorical eternity. And then it happened again.

This time she didn't miss it. There was no way she could, because it happened right in front of her.

The box of chocolate cookies was laying on the coffee table. And suddenly, while Minnie watched in amazement, the box moved. It didn't change its position by much (which was clearly how she'd missed it the first time), but it did shift from where it had been. It had been lying next to Keith's balled-up note that explained where he and Earl had gone. Now the cookie box bumped the note, which in turn rolled a few inches across the table top.

Minnie gaped wide at the cookie box. She didn't know what to think. Maybe, maybe . . .

But then, as if to help her make up her mind on what she was witnessing, the cookie box completely flipped over and upended its contents onto the small table.

Minnie leapt up from her chair and backed away towards the bed. From a position by the foot of the bed, she watched the cookie box carefully, to see what it would do next.

But it did nothing; it was just a cookie box again.

Minnie realized that she'd been holding her breath from sheer apprehension. Now she relaxed again. Not for the first time, she wondered what sort of ghosthunter she was that got scared so easily. *Herman too remarked as much last night.*

She had almost managed to smile at her own timidity, when the bathroom door clicked open of its own accord.

Oh shit! No, Minnie had not missed anything this time. She'd seen exactly what had happened. Just like that time when the toilet had seemingly flushed itself, the door handle had twisted itself and then the door had opened up.

And then just to make certain she understood what was going on, the door swung inward and clicked shut again.

Oh, my dear God, the poltergeists are back again! Keith! Earl! Where the heck are both of you!?

By now Minnie knew she wasn't alone in the hotel room. There were unseen presences, people in here with her. She tried to recall what

Earl had said about the Jerome Grand Hotel's ghosts. Hadn't he insisted that the spirits were merely mischievous and not malicious? Hadn't Earl said that for the most part the Jerome Grand Hotel ghosts were playfully benign and not out to hurt anyone?

At the moment Minnie didn't believe that at all. A sudden panic was filling her up, and her already agitated state of mind was only further agitated a moment later, when something flew at her. The airborne object came from her left. She caught sight of it out of the corner of her eye and ducked in time. It sailed over her and crashed into the back of the chair she'd just been sitting on. She finally got a proper look at it: an empty beer can Keith had left on the nightstand.

She couldn't stare too long, however, as something else had already been flung at her by the room's unseen presences. This time it was the portable hair dryer she'd brought along with her. She threw herself down on the bed. The dryer zipped past her and hit the upended cookie box, which had so far retained a precarious unbalanced position on the coffee table after discarding its contents. Now, both cookie box and hair dryer hit the floor on the other side of the table.

By now other objects were flying through the air at random and Minnie decided that the bed wasn't the safest place to be. So, she quickly scooted off of it and ducked into the nook between the nightstand on that side and the wall.

Once she was safely out of harm's way (so long as nothing got thrown down at that portion of the floor), the poltergeists in the room really went to town. Seemingly everything in the room became airborne, including at one point, the bed rising a few inches off the floor. Objects were zipping through the air at different speeds. Some of them (like a matching pair of wine glasses) shattered violently and made equally violent sounds, while others, like all of the pillows, flew through the air like clouds, and finally piled themselves in a corner beneath the TV.

Minnie huddled in her nook and felt terrified. She'd never seen anything like this before.

And concurrent with the start of this really crazy poltergeist activity, she'd also felt the return of that cold wind from her previous poltergeist encounter. The wind had swirled around her twice and then blown away, once more towards the bathroom door.

Minnie wanted to flee to safety outside in the corridor, but there was too much flying debris in the way. She didn't even care that she was only wearing her panties; if she'd been granted the chance to make it out of the room naked, she would have taken it. But no, even such an embarrassing nudist escape wasn't going to happen here. Each time she made a move to get to her feet, something else would come flying toward her and she would be forced back down in the corner, to cower there until this airborne insanity was over.

By now most objects in the room had been displaced to some degree or other. Alone in being unaffected was the television. Even the window drapes had been wrenched sideways and finally rolled up and cast up onto the curtain rods. Magazines zipped across the room like aircraft. The detached soap dish from the bathroom ricocheted off surface after surface, making deep dents in the wall with each impact.

Minnie just stared and watched the spirits wreck the hotel room.

Benevolent? harmless? Benign? This lot? Earl must be out of his damn mind!

Whether by accident or design (just to taunt her with her helplessness), Minnie's cellphone, which had also been a part of the airborne commotion, had landed on the bed. Once Minnie noticed it lying there, she wasted no time in snatching it up and dialing Keith. This was purely a reflex action on her part, total survival mode, an action taken before her mind had had the time to process the fact that the phone wouldn't be working, its malfunction due to the same unseen creatures that were currently terrorizing her.

"Hello! Hello! Keith!" she yelled into the phone, then flung it onto the bed, collapsed back into her safe corner and began crying.

And as if the whole point of trashing the hotel room was simply to reduce Minnie to tears, that was when the energetic poltergeist activity began to settle down.

***

It was a while though before the turmoil completely subsided. Minnie did what she had all along; she simply waited, while her terror over the supernatural manifestation slowly became relief that it was ending.

True, she was unhurt, but she felt traumatized.

Finally, she felt safe enough to get to her feet. Once standing upright again, she waited a few seconds to make sure that the poltergeists weren't playing possum. But no, the spirits appeared to have left the room; she got no sense of having company in here anymore, nor did she feel the preternatural cold of their accompanying wind.

The hotel room seemed turned upside-down, not through breakage—though whatever was made of glass now lay in shards at one point or the other—but simply because everything was now piled up over one another without rhyme or reason. Even the clothes that had hung in the closet now lay draped over other things. Two Ouija boards lay side-by-side near the miraculously unharmed TV. Of the boards' planchettes, there was no sign.

Taking care to avoid stepping on any glass shards, Minnie hastily assembled an outfit of jeans and blouse. When she was dressed, she located a pair of shoes and pulled them on. Then she grabbed up her phone from where she'd dropped it, picked up her purse, and then hurried over to the door and slipped outside.

Once outside in the corridor, she heaved a massive sigh of relief. The calm orderliness out here made her think she'd imagined the crazy disarray in her room, but a glance back through the door reassured her that such was not the case.

She locked the door.

What do I do now? The best thing is to inform the girl in reception of what just happened. Then, while they clean the room up, I'm heading into town to look for Keith and Earl. Those guys ain't ever gonna believe what happened to me while they were out sightseeing. Hey, I'm forgetting something!

She got the room key out of her purse and reopened the door. Then she got her cellphone out of her purse too, tapped over to the camera app, and video-recorded the mess in the room. She figured that once the hotel janitors and maids got over the shock of seeing what had occurred in here, they'd get right to work on cleaning things up, which meant that without video evidence, she'd otherwise be unable to prove her story was true.

She reviewed the phone video. Thankfully it was okay, with just a hint of waviness in it.

Okay, now that I've gotten proof, I need to get out of this horrible building for a while. I hope my phone works once I'm down in the town.

But while shutting the door again, she'd been feeling odd. It wasn't a similar 'odd' to when the poltergeist wind had been blowing, but still . . . she had the same feeling of not being alone.

Fearing the poltergeist spirits had returned for a replay, and wondering exactly what was left in the room for them to throw around, she quickly pulled the door shut and leaned against the hallway wall to catch a relieved breath before heading for the elevator.

But then she noticed the old man standing at the end of the corridor, about two yards away. The man was old, and had a rugged look to him, with a long scraggly beard and deep-set gray eyes. He was wearing old-time clothes that were not exactly ragged but seemed a bit threadbare. A sort of aura of death seemed to blow from him down the corridor.

Oh no, not again! It's the miner!

Hotel legend had it that the ghost of a long dead miner often appeared on this floor, but so far none of them had seen him. Nor, seemingly, had anyone else rooming in the hotel at this time.

Minnie quailed before the phantom. *Why me? Why the hell does it have to be me who's witnessing all of this crazy phenomena? Why not the guys? And where the hell have they gotten to anyway?*

She couldn't help her fright. This old man now watching her was long dead, no doubt about it. No one dressed like that nowadays; and besides, his eyes were as lifeless as those of a cooked fish.

And then he began moving towards her. 'Moving,' because he wasn't walking. No, just like in the movies, the ghost was sliding along the floor towards her, coming on slowly at first but with his speed increasing perceptibly by the moment.

Minnie panicked. No, she wasn't about to let the ghost get a hold of her.

She spun around and ran for the opposite end of the corridor.

She intended to knock on Nancy's door and hide in her room. She prayed hard that either Nancy or Herman was in. But then suddenly she heard the noise of the ancient Otis elevator in the middle of the corridor arriving, and she changed her mind. Why hide, when she was on her way outside anyway? Once outside, she would be free of the aggressive ghosts. The stairs were beside the elevator, and she could have run down them instead, but she realized that in her panic, she might topple down them and break her neck.

So, she ran for the elevator. She looked back once, saw that the miner was gaining on her with his no-steps slide, and increased her speed. The elevator had now opened and an elderly woman in very fashionable but also very outdated white clothes was just getting out of it. Once outside of the elevator cage, the woman remained standing beside the elevator, smiling at Minnie.

"Excuse me!" Minnie gasped and ducked around the elderly lady.

Minnie spun around inside the elevator and with an index finger punched the button for the lobby. The elevator didn't move. The she remembered she needed to insert the elevator key, and quickly located it on the hotel key ring.

Oh, damn this archaic self-service machine!

After a desperate peek outside revealed that the sliding old miner was almost at the elevator, Minnie stuck the elevator key into its keyhole and quickly turned the key. There, she was good to go now. But then she realized that she'd merely panicked; she only required the elevator key to access the top three floors, she didn't need it for either of the lower two floors: the restaurant and the lobby, and the lobby was where she was headed.

But before the elevator would leave this floor, she still needed to shut both its outer glass door and its inner metal grate. After a further peek outside revealed the miner was almost on her now, she grabbed hold of handle of the glass door and tried to pull it shut, but the door didn't move. Minnie tried again and still couldn't get it to close. The grate seemed even more immobile. Would the elevator work with its doors opened? The notice on the doors said it wouldn't, but Minnie was desperate enough to try it anyway. She punched the lobby button and got no response. She knew that by now the miner must have reached the elevator cage, and that any moment she would feel his cold clammy fingers on her warm flesh. She began punching the lobby button in a panic.

The elderly woman in white hadn't left yet. She was staring into the cage with a concerned look, as if wondering what Minnie's rush was. Or maybe she thought Minnie was on drugs.

Then Minnie had a sudden sense of matter dispersing nearby. She peeked back out into the corridor again and saw that the miner was gone. She heaved a sigh of relief, but not for long, because the woman was now peeking in at her.

"Are you alright, sweetie?" the lady in white asked. "You look like you've seen . . ."

"Yes, I'm fine, but . . ."

But Minnie had already realized that there was something 'wrong' about this woman too, whose white clothes now seemingly reeked of mildew, like she'd only recently unearthed them from an ancient crypt. The woman's eyes held the same lifeless energy that the vanished miner's had. Minnie realized that she too was a ghost.

Oh no, she's one of them too!

She grabbed a hold of the glass door's handle again and tried to slide it to the right, but it still didn't respond. The glass door stubbornly refused to move.

"Well, you don't seem alright to me," the woman said, stepping inside the cage. "Here, darling, let me give you a hand with the cage controls."

Minnie had had enough. "No, no, don't you dare come in here!" she shrieked at the top of her voice. "Don't you dare come near me!" The woman's smell of ancient decay was seemingly all around her now, as if Minnie herself had been mistaken for dead and interred alive.

"Well, well, well, I was only trying to be helpful," the woman in white said angrily. "And you don't have to be so rude, you know. That's the problem with kids nowadays, no manners at all. No manners at all." She stood there for a while longer just inside the entrance to the cage, staring angrily in at Minnie, and then said mildly: "Well, sweetie, if you don't want my help with the elevator, I'll just leave you alone then."

And then, with the same kind of 'implosive' noise that had accompanied the miner's vanishing, the elderly woman and her reek of decaying clothes vanished too.

Minnie struggled to get the elevators doors shut again, and when they still didn't respond, she slumped down to the floor of the cage and began weeping again.

CHAPTER 10

Herman and Nancy had been preparing to go out to town. Herman figured they would have a late breakfast at one of the picturesque ghost-themed diners on Main Street; and once there, he would finally have his romantic one-on-one talk with Nancy.

"Thanks for suggesting this," Nancy said as they stepped out of her hotel room. "I do need to get out of this place today. Last night was such a—"

"Shush!" Herman silenced her with a finger over her lips. "Do you hear that? Sounds like a woman crying."

"Yes, I do," Nancy said after a moment's listening. After staring left and right down the empty corridor, she said: "Herman, I think the sounds coming from the elevator!"

Herman too looked over towards the elevator, which was only a short distance from both of their hotel rooms. Yes, it sounded like the crying woman was in there.

"Come on," he told Nancy. "Let's go find out what's wrong."

Together, he and Nancy hurried over towards the elevator.

"Hey, I think it's Minnie, from yesterday," Nancy said when they reached the elevator.

And yes, it was Minnie Connors in there. She was slumped in a heap on the floor of the elevator, beneath the controls, and was weeping her eyes out.

Minnie looked up at them from the floor of the cage. Her reaction surprised Herman. At first, she seemed not to recognize them at all. She flinched at the sight of them, and then retreated several yards further into the deep old-fashioned cage, where she now huddled tightly in the corner as if she was trying to force her way through its walls. But then the light of recognition shone in her eyes and she relaxed.

"What the hell happened to you?" Herman demanded in an alarmed voice. Minnie didn't seem to be hurt; which was a relief, but she seemed completely terrified.

"Oh, Herman, don't address her that harshly; can't you see she's scared?" Nancy said. "Something's scared the wits out of her." Nancy entered the elevator and walked over to Minnie. She knelt beside the distraught young woman and tried to comfort her.

"Minnie, what happened to you?" she asked.

"My . . . my . . . gho-gho-gho . . . in-in . . . gho . . ." Minnie stuttered back.

Nancy looked up at Herman. "I don't like the looks of this. Give me a hand and let's get her into my room and put her in bed."

Herman sighed and stepped into the elevator cage and walked over to the two women. Today was already taking a turn for the unpredictable. As he bent over Minnie and helped pull her up, he had the clear impression that his romantic date with Nancy had just been torpedoed again.

Well, maybe tonight then, if we can—

But then, just as they'd both gotten Minnie standing on her feet again, Herman heard the elevator grate closing behind them. He looked over his shoulder and saw the folded metal gate purposefully sliding sideways on its own until it shut. In similar fashion, the elevator's exterior glass door was also closing of its own accord. His surprise was so great that he almost let go of Minnie.

"Hey, careful with her, man!" Nancy scolded him. "And, why did you shut the doors after you? We aren't going downstairs yet."

Herman realized that Nancy hadn't yet realized that the doors had closed on their own. "I didn't shut them. They just shut on their own."

That got Nancy's attention. She looked at the closed grate, then looked at the elevator buttons. Herman looked at the buttons too. They both saw the 'Lobby' button click down and remain locked in place, in its active position.

Nancy stared open-mouthed at Herman, and he could read the fear in her eyes. "Herman, I thought you said that you didn't . . ."

"No, I didn't," Herman agreed.

"Help me hold her!" he next told Nancy and abruptly shifted the entirety of Minnie's weight onto her. It was fortunate that by now Minnie had regained some of her self-possession, or both she and Nancy would have collapsed to the floor again.

Once he found himself unburdened, Herman dashed over to the control panel. He quickly pressed the red 'Stop' button. The elevator hadn't moved yet, and Herman was suddenly desperate that it remained up here on the third floor. However, the 'Stop' control button didn't seem to be working today.

"Maybe you should just let it go down to the lobby," Nancy suggested.

Herman shook his head at her. "Hell no, Nancy! I don't know why, but I've a feeling that'll be a real bad idea."

Herman began pushing each cage control, anything to make the 'Lobby' button pop back up again. Even without the button having depressed itself, he knew something was wrong because in normal usage the button never stayed down; how it worked was that you depressed it for two seconds to start the cage moving, and then when you took your finger away, it returned to its default position. But now? Herman couldn't get that chilling click as the lobby control had locked into its current position—like the snapping of bones in a hanged man's neck—out of his mind. What had that click been? Surely not . . . in a panic he stared at the cables visible through the gaps in the upper part of the cage walls. Surely . . .

All Herman understood, was that, no matter whatever else happened right now, he needed to ensure the elevator cage remained up here on the third floor. He turned Minnie's elevator key in the keyhole and tried to make the cage lift rather than descend. He had the feeling of a very clear and present danger. He had no idea what Minnie had experienced in here, but for it to have reduced her to the sniveling condition in which they had found her, it must have been really bad.

Then it occurred to him that he could stall the elevator's descent by opening either of its two doors. There was no way the cage would move if he could get one of the doors open.

Why didn't I think of that earlier!?

Herman grabbed the grip of the steel grate and tried to shift it. It didn't move. He tugged against it. It seemed set in steel. He exerted himself again, but the grate remained in place. With the sense of a clock somewhere ticking away to a horrible doom, he reached through the grate, located the handle of the outer door, and pulled that to the left instead. No dice there either.

Herman felt defeated. He suddenly had the sense that something had control of the elevator cage, and that that something wasn't particularly friendly.

Then he felt a tap on his shoulder and on turning around, saw that Nancy and Minnie had now joined him by the elevator door.

"Then who? . . . Maybe a malfunction?" Nancy questioned, her eyes full of fright and panic.

Herman stared back helplessly at her.

"The gho-gho-gho . . . the ghosts did it!" Minnie yelped.

But by then the elevator was already in motion again. And rather than descending at its normal slow pace, it was plummeting downward at speed, as if the elevator cables that held it steady had all snapped at the same time.

Herman hugged the two women tight and braced himself for a very bad crash.

CHAPTER 11

After a few drinks Keith had begun to come to terms with being trapped in the past. He was still bothered by his situation, but was able to rationalize things by telling himself it would only be for a short time.

Something didn't make sense however. While buying a drink, Keith had seen his reflection in the mirror that backed the drinks cabinet. To his surprise he still looked like himself. Before seeing his reflection back there he'd imagined that he might be temporarily 'visiting' the past in someone else's body.

But no, I'm apparently here in person. In the flesh, as it were. Now that's odd. How can that have happened?

But with no answer to his question, for the moment Keith had to content him with enjoying what the past had to offer, while of course trying to find his way back home to the future. Because, dammit, the past was simply so primitive.

Take for instance this bar he was drinking in. The place was like a backwoods shack that some shyster had hurriedly erected to make as many quick bucks as possible. It was hard to determine which was filthier; the establishment or its mining clientele. The men were mostly dirty and seemed to have come straight here from work. Intense odors kept assaulting Keith's nostrils, some identifiable, some not. Every nose-offending smell you'd encounter in a modern truck stop and then more.

Keith was sitting at a table with four other men. Two of the men had women on their laps, while the other two were arm wrestling. It was brutal arm wrestling too, the sort with razor blades stuck in a block beneath both contestant's forearms, ready to draw blood from whoever lost; which arrangement made little sense to Keith, seeing as the winner wouldn't be able to work the mines for a while. And yet each of the two contestants had several nasty scars on the back of his arm as testament that this wasn't his first dance.

Around Keith and his seated companions, a group had slowly formed, with men placing bets on who would win, while flirty waitresses hustled their way through the press with fresh drinks.

The men struggled in their deadly contest, with each of them forcing the other's arm down towards the razors placed to slice them open. But, realizing what was at stake here, the contest wasn't about to be decided yet.

Keith soon tired of watching the men. Apparently, the last time they'd arm wrestled, it had gone on for two hours. Cody, the hairier and uglier man had won. And Joey, the only slightly less hairy and ugly man had won their previous encounter.

Crazy, crazy, crazy.

Keith got up and ordered another drink. This time he carried the tankard outside the bar and sat on a wine barrel taking in the sights. Directly across the road from him, two drunks were having a fight while men and women egged them on. Inebriated as both combatants were, their fight was more comic relief than anything else, and the fight shortly ended in fittingly absurdist manner, when both men fell into a large puddle of mud, whereupon both seemed to forget they'd been fighting and began floundering about like they were drowning, which led to them both needing to be rescued by their equally drunken friends.

A horse-drawn carriage full of beer kegs pulled up in front of the drunks across the street, obscuring them from view. Keith hadn't yet worked out what year this was. It seemed to him that it would be weird to inquire about the date from someone, and so far neither of the two drinking places he'd stepped into had had a calendar on the walls. He had the feeling that this was somewhere around the turn of the century, but whether he was in the late nineteenth or early twentieth was still a mystery to him.

Dammit, Earl would give his right arm to see all this! Keith though. *To regress back in time like I'm doing now would be worth a million dollars to him. Well, if nothing else, being here like this is sure to give me inspiration for a few new paintings.*

Keith finished his beer, and decided to take a walk. The Crib District (or 'Husband's Alley') extended into the distance and he was still at the start of the street.

He began walking, staring curiously left and right while attempting to look like he wasn't doing so. He wasn't interested in hiring a woman for the night, though he passed several who were very pretty, particularly two girls whom he saw fanning themselves outside of his reputed grandaunt Nora Brown's place. He walked past her brothel with a smile on his face. Nora Brown was a plain-looking plump brunette. She was standing on the front porch and welcoming her male clients.

"Okay, boys, Now I know I ain't much ta look at myself," she was saying with an avaricious smile," but once you see the girls I've got in here for ya lovin', y'all gonna love me more than you do ya own sweet mothers."

Keith laughed and walked. Yeah, granny, was doing alright for herself. He didn't dare go closer for a better look at her, because he didn't wish to be himself mistaken for a client and pulled through those front saloon doors.

What in the world am I gonna tell Minnie if that happened?

Thinking of Minnie made Keith pause for thought. He wondered what she was up to. For a moment he felt panic that he might be trapped here in the past forever and might never see Minnie again.

Nah, never fear. I'll get out of here somehow. But . . . maybe I should just make a baby with Minnie like she wants me to. That way, if I ever went away suddenly, or if I just died all of a sudden, she wouldn't be all alone, she'd as least have the kid. But having a child is gonna be a huge adjustment for me to make—the demands of having a kid is certain to wreak havoc on my creativity . . . Hey, who's that?

Keith had just caught sight of a brunette woman. For a brief moment the woman's head had flashed into sight in the window of a small house across the road, then vanished again.

The woman's head didn't reappear, but that brief glimpse of her had been enough to make Keith change direction and start walking over there. The brunette had looked scared of something, and Keith couldn't be sure, but it had also seemed as if someone had his hands around her neck.

After talking a few steps, Keith broke into a brisk run. The house he was heading for wasn't a shack. It wasn't one of the many 'cribs' that adorned the street, but then, it also wasn't as large as the other brothel buildings. It was set a little back from the road, and once Keith hit the opposite sidewalk, he dashed around a few drunks who didn't realize a woman might be in trouble just a few feet from where they sat drinking.

"Hey, watch where you're damn goin'!" someone yelled after him.

Keith ran on. Soon he'd reached the window where he'd seen the woman, and, convention and modesty be damned, was peeking in.

The woman in the room was still alive, but barely just. His second view of her revealed both that she was strikingly beautiful, and also that she was seconds away from death by strangulation.

"I already warned you, Sammie, you dirty bitch. It ain't over 'tween us till I says so!" the man strangling her was saying.

The strangler was a miner, a hairy guy with a beard that reminded Keith of former president Lincoln. He had a crazed look in his eyes and his lips were twisted together in an enraged snarl. Both of the man's hands were tightly fastened around the brunette prostitute's neck, and were throttling her tighter and tighter, while she beat against his hairy arms. 'Sammie' as he'd called her had tears in her eyes and a pathetic pleading look on her face. Her face was already turning blue and Keith knew he had to act quickly or she'd soon be gone for good.

"Hey, what'cha think you're doing ta her!?" Keith yelled through the window. "Let go of that woman, ya darn fool!"

The man froze and looked toward the window. An expression of panic began replacing the rage on his face. "This ain't what it looks like."

"Yeah," Keith said. "You're strangling her as a favor. Goddamn let go of her neck!"

But unfortunately, the crazy miner still wasn't letting go of Sammie yet; who was now choking away like her life would end in the next ten seconds. The man's hairy hands were still locked around her throat and he seemed unable to get it through his drunken head that she was almost dead.

With this being the case, Keith now saw no other responsible course of action to take than to leap up and pull himself into bedroom through its open window. From where he stood on the outside of the house, he could see no door and he had no idea of the layout of the house, or of how long it would take him to locate and reach this same bedroom, which would most likely only be explained to him after he'd first taken the time to explain to the building's other residents that a murder was being committed inside their home.

So, he hauled himself in through the bedroom window, dropped to the floor and charged at the strangler. When the man saw Keith coming for him, he panicked and finally let go of Sammie. She toppled backwards onto Keith, who grabbed her before she fell to the floor.

The killer instantly bolted. Keith was left along with the brunette prostitute. He quickly laid her out on her bed and tried to revive her.

"Hey, Sammie, wake up!" Keith told her. "You're okay now! He's left!"

But he quickly realized that his rescue attempt had been too late. Sammie was dead. Her tongue, fat and swollen, protruded from her blue face like a disgusting slug.

Keith stared at her in horror and blinked away tears. Oh no! Now, he remembered who she had to be: Sammie Dean, strangled to death and her murder never solved. Looking quickly around, he saw Sammie's pet German shepherd was also in the room. The dog lay asleep by a wall, its limbs arranged in a careless way that made Keith realize it had been drugged.

Well, I KNOW who killed Sammie Dean and, seeing as I'm stuck here for the time being, I'm gonna get the police onto that guy and have him put behind bars.

But then, Keith began hearing voices outside of the bedroom door. He paused to listen:

"Yeah, he's in there. I'm telling ya!" someone said.

"Hey, Jon, are you sure Sammie's really dead?"

"Yeah, yeah, I'm sure. She and I was having a l'il friendly conversation and next thing I know this crazed-lookin' fellow climbs in through the window, shoves me into a corner and then strangles her."

"And you just sat there and let him kill Sammie, you idiot?"

"Nah, nah, not willingly. But he hit me with something. Look, my forehead's still bleedin.' He knocked out Sammie's dog too."

Keith groaned. *Oh, no, that idiot is trying to frame me for the murder he's just committed.*

Keith realized that if he was found in here with the corpse, he'd have a hard time proving his innocence. He needed to get outside of the house again before the people talking entered the bedroom and either caught him or saw him clearly enough to later identify him to the cops.

Keith sighed down at the dead woman, who had her eyes open and was staring at the ceiling. But he didn't the time to wait and close her eyes. Instead, he turned and ran over to the window.

In theory, getting out of the room should have been easier than getting in. But something went wrong. As Keith was climbing out of the window, he suddenly found he'd lost his footing on the sill, and he slipped back inside again.

That unfortunate slipup was all it took. The next moment the room was full of angry people who were yelling and pointing at him.

"Git 'im, git that darn bastard! Don't let 'im git away!"

The enraged mob split into two parts; the women rushed towards the dead prostitute on the bed, while the men, with Sammie's murderer at the head of the pack, rushed towards Keith. He felt himself grabbed from behind and pulled back into the room.

"I didn't do it!" he yelled as fists began to pummel him. "It wasn't me! It was—!"

But something hit the back of Keith's head then, and he was knocked out cold before he could reveal who the real murderer was.

CHAPTER 12

The elevator crash, when it occurred, was worse that Herman had expected. It seemed a cliché, but time really did seem to slow down during the second or so when the elevator cage dropped in freefall from the third floor.

During that split-second eternity, Herman gripped Nancy and Minnie tightly and hoped for the best. In reality, a three-floor drop wasn't one that ought to kill them, but in this case, the elevator seemed to have a diabolical plan of its own and this made their survival doubtful.

Bang! The cage hit down in the lobby. There was a moment when all three of them were thrown off of their feet, and then space seemed to warp around Herman in a way that he didn't understand.

But when he finally felt able to sit up again, he looked around in shock.

Where is this? he thought on seeing his new surroundings.

He wasn't alone here either. Both Nancy and Minnie were also in the same space. All three of them were lying on the floor in a cramped little room that was fenced off by a half-cage on one side. The room smelt of oil and also contained a lot of machinery and . . .

"Oh, where the hell are we now?" Nancy said, while also sitting up. She began feeling herself all over for broken bones, and Herman started doing the same too. He still felt stunned by the impact, but was more stunned by what was clearly some form of spatial transference here. *It's like the elevator brought us here—wherever this is—for a reason.*

"Is it all over now?" Minnie asked, sitting up also. Then she gave a loud scream and pointed. "Look, look, look!"

Herman had been relieved to find that he wasn't hurt in any way. But when he saw what had just agitated Minnie again, his relief immediately departed.

There was a man lying on the floor, a short distance away. That the man was dead was incontrovertible; his head was stuck underneath . . .

It took Herman a few seconds to understand what they were all looking at. It simply required a shift of perspective and then their new location made sense to him.

"You know, I think we've somehow been transported . . ." he searched his mind for the sci-fi word. "Translocated, is it? We've been shifted in space to the back side of the elevator. The 'elevator room' it's probably called."

"Who the fuck is that?" Minnie asked, moving away from the corpse. "He looks dead!"

"Calm down, everyone," Herman said as calmly as he could manage. "First of all, let's all get to our feet." He waited till everyone was standing up, then went on speaking: "Okay, first things first. What's most important now is that we're all still alive and all unhurt."

"I suppose that means the elevator just wanted to bring us down here," Nancy said, moving to Herman's side and slipping an arm around him. "It never meant us any harm."

"Sure, didn't seem that way to me up there," Minnie said, stepping close to Herman and Nancy. "Listen, what do we do about this dead guy? And did the elevator kill him or what?"

Herman scratched his chin. "That, I don't know." He studied the dead man for a moment, then walked closer for a better look. For a guy whose head was stuck beneath an elevator cage, there was very little blood on display, but Herman reasoned this was because most of the trauma would be to the corpse's head, and so the blood was more likely to have collected on the ground beneath the cage.

Herman knelt down and prodded the corpse a bit, then got back to his feet and turned around to face the two women. "Okay, from the looks of this guy, he's probably the elevator maintenance man. Now, we've either of two options. Firstly, we can simply find a working phone and call the cops . . ."

Minnie immediately held up a finger. "Hold on there for just a minute." Once Herman nodded and ceased speaking, she rummaged around in her purse and got out her cellphone. "Not working as usual," she said in disgust after a look at the phone's screen. "Dammit, I was hoping we'd get a signal in here."

"What's our second plan of action?" Nancy asked, while still clinging tightly to Herman in a way that he liked.

"We leave here and find someone in management and tell them their elevator maintenance guy just got killed . . . again."

That made Nancy look oddly at him. "Again?" she asked in surprise.

Herman nodded. "Yeah, sure. I don't recall the details, but I do know that about eighty years or so ago, a guy—don't recall his name either—wound up with his head stuck under the elevator in similar fashion. The case was never—hey, Minnie what's the matter?"

Minnie was staring goggle-eyed at the floor. "Are you sure this dead guy isn't that dead guy?" she asked.

Herman looked at her askance. "What are you talking about?"

She sighed and slowly regained her composure. "Well, it's just that I've been seeing ghosts since I woke up, and I'm very sure this is simply another one of them."

"Ghosts?" Herman laughed. "Oh, come on now, be serious."

Minnie shook her head. "No, *you* be serious." While keeping her eyes fixed on Herman, she violently jerked her finger down at the dead man. "You keep acting like there's no things like ghosts, but you're wrong."

"No, I'm right," Herman insisted. "The dead are dead; they never come back."

"So, how do you explain us all somehow winding up here?" Minnie asked. "I'm almost scared that we all died in the elevator crash and this is hell."

"We didn't fall far enough to die," Herman countered her. "Okay, I'll admit that I don't know how we got out of the elevator to this rear area, but that in no way means that ghosts now exist. And, and . . ."

"Don't bother, Herman," Nancy said, in a soft, frightened voice. "Minnie's right. Look! See for yourself!"

While arguing, Herman had been staring at Minnie and Minnie had been staring at Herman, and neither of them had been staring at the dead man. They both did so now, only to discover that he was no longer there. Yes, the corpse with its head wedged under the elevator cage had now completely vanished. And at that moment a hotel guest must have called the old Otis elevator to one of the upper floors, because the elevator cage began rising in its chamber, which allowed all three of them to see that there was nothing in the space it had vacated. No remnants of mangled flesh, no splattered brains, and no blood either.

Herman looked at Nancy. "Okay now, I guess I do believe in ghosts," he said.

He couldn't explain how he felt; this was just too incredible.

Minnie stepped up to his side and took hold of his arm. "Please, let's get out of this creepy place," she pleaded earnestly.

"Honey, do you mean the hotel, or the damn town?" Nancy asked in a sardonic voice. "I'm starting to feel like I've had more than enough of both of 'em."

Herman was feeling funny too. He nodded to both women and led the way to the farther end of the room, where a door opened out into the bowels of the building from where they quickly found their way, thankfully unnoticed, back to the livable areas of the hotel.

CHAPTER 13

On stepping back into the lobby with Herman and Nancy, Minnie noticed Earl returning through the hotel's front doors.

Earl looked very worried. Minnie excused herself from her companions and hurried over to him.

"What's the matter with you?" she asked him. "And where's Keith?"

"I don't where Keith is," Earl said. "He's gone missing."

Minnie's eyes narrowed. Not for the first time today, she felt both frightened and angry. "Earl, what do you mean, he's gone missing? You two went out together, didn't you?"

Earl nodded and looked confused. "Yes, yes, we did. We went to Jerome Avenue; you remember that area, don't you? Around the old-time Crib District?"

"Yes, yes. And what happened when you got there?"

Earl sighed. "I really don't know. Keith and I were gonna do a spook stakeout on the street on a hunch I had yesterday. We'd each picked one side of the street to keep an eye on. So, my bro crosses the road and then he simply vanishes into thin air."

"What do you mean? How could he vanish into thin air?"

"I dunno. I saw it with my own eyes and I don't believe it. I've been looking all around that area for the past two hours, entering every single shop there and enquiring if they've seen him. But no one has. So, I finally gave up the search and came back to the hotel. Listen, I'm bushed. I walked all the way to town and back again. I gotta go take a rest upstairs before I resume the search for Keith."

Shaking his head, Earl turned and walked off towards the elevator. Minnie watched him leave. For a moment she thought of hurrying after

Earl and warning him about the elevator. But then she decided not to. If the machine wanted to have its evil fun with him too, then let it. So far today, she'd been scared out of her wits at least three times. And it was all Earl's fault for bringing her here.

And now her boyfriend had inexplicably gone missing too, and Minnie was certain that that too was Earl's fault in some way.

Once the elevator had closed behind Earl, Minnie walked back over to Herman and Nancy to inform them of this latest development.

Of course, both were as surprised as she was to learn of Keith's sudden vanishing. Herman and Minnie had been intending to go out for a walk, but now they decided to put it off till another time.

For now, however, they and Minnie headed for the bar. They all needed something to steady their nerves.

CHAPTER 14

Keith awoke slowly and then the headache hit him. While coming to terms with the dizzying pain, he slowly remembered why his head now hurt.

Those blasted idiots thought I was the one who'd strangled Sammie Dean! They cracked me in the head while I was trying to climb out of the window. Where am I now? The sheriff's office?

But no, this definitely wasn't a sheriff's office. In fact, it looked more like a hospital room. Keith tried to sit up, but found that he was strapped down on a gurney at the side of a room that looked like an old operating theater, with a long bed or table in its center, a surgical lighting arrangement overhead, and several machines humming alongside cream-colored walls.

Keith's spirits fell at the realization that he was in an operating theater.

Those drunks must have wounded me pretty badly for me to have been brought in here, he thought. But if that's the case, where are the doctors and nurses and interns who're supposed to attend to me?

His clothes had once more changed. At some point on the way here, his regular garb had been stripped off of him and had been replaced a light blue hospital gown.

The door at the far end of the operating theater was open and he could see outside of it into what seemed to be a corridor or a hallway. But for the moment at least, he saw no sign of the people who were supposed to treat his injury.

The first thing I gotta do once the doctors get here is clear my name and point out the real killer to the police, before he slips out of town. Him getting away might make things difficult for—

At that moment, a sudden, loud piercing noise both ended Keith's rational consideration of his strange situation and also made his head hurt. The noise had come from somewhere outside on his left.

The noise came again, and it was on this repeat that Keith realized he was hearing a woman screaming. Keith felt the blood run cold in his veins.

What the hell?

Then there followed a third loud scream, one that halfway through abruptly transformed into a bloodcurdling gurgle, as if someone had cut the woman's throat and now she was gurgling her blood away. This horrible sound slowly dwindled to silence.

By now Keith was wrestling against his bonds. To his mind there had been something completely unnatural about that scream. In his experience there were screams and then there were *screams*, as in expressions of pain that transcended normal experience; and the noises made by the screaming woman down the hospital corridor, fit securely into the latter category of misery.

All of a sudden Keith felt he needed to be well away from this clinic or wherever this was, before its medical staff showed up. His resolution was helped by another set of screams, these ones clearly male, from the opposite, right side of the corridor. If anything, these masculine screams were even more horrifying that the woman's had been.

What on earth are they doing to these people in here? Where am I—a secret government interrogation facility?

Keith Roche now gave getting free his full attention. He was bound by three sets of straps, one around his ankles, one around his chest and the third and tightest around his waist; this lattermost one being the most problematic to escape because it was the one holding down his forearms to his sides.

Alas, he discovered he was too late anyway. Just as he felt the leather strap holding him down around the waist start to give, he heard the sound of squeaky wheels approaching. Keith tensed, and waited to see who was coming.

A nurse shortly walked into the room. She was young and pretty, and was pushing a medical cart ahead of her.

She smiled when she saw he was awake. She steered her instrument-and-medicines-laden cart over to the operating table and then walked over to look down at Keith.

"Welcome back to the land of the living, Mr. Roche," she said.

The fact that she knew his name surprised Keith, but then he decided it was only to be expected.

"Please listen to me," he said urgently, his words coming in a rush, because he knew he needed to be heard in full before he suffered the same fate as the unfortunates in those nearby rooms. "I know what you folks is all thinkin' but you're dead wrong. It wasn't me that killed that woman back there—Sammie Dean—No, lady, I ain't the one who killed Sammie."

The nurse nodded sympathetically. "Oh? So, who killed the prostitute then?"

"T'was another guy there; a miner with a beard like Abe Lincoln. He's the one that did it."

The nurse laughed. "Oh, you're referring to Mr. Jonathan?"

"What's so funny?"

The nurse's mirth immediately vanished. "Mr. Jonathan and ten different witness all swear that they saw you kill Miss Dean."

"But that ain't true! I'd nothing to do with it at all. I even tried to save her . . ."

He shut up because the young woman clearly didn't believe a word he was saying. Suddenly he understood her reasoning: she obviously sympathized with the victim, because they were both about the same age, and maybe she had a secret fantasy of living a similar 'dirty and sexy' life; something she'd never dare act out in real life. And as such, to her, a man like himself, who would summarily end such a daring fantasized life was the lowest of the low.

The nurse smiled. "Anyway, Mr. Roche, welcome to the Jerome Asylum for the Criminally Insane."

"The *where?*"

She leaned over him. "You've been judged as criminally insane, Mr. Roche, and we're here to treat you."

"What sorta treatment is you talking 'bout?"

She smiled again. "You're to be lobotomized, Mr. Roche."

"Lobotomized? That's like when they butcher ya in the brains, ain't it?"

"Yes, and I don't see why not. According to police investigations, your fingerprints have been found at the sites of six other murders of young prostitutes."

"But that's bullcrap!" Keith screamed, suddenly beside himself with anger. "I ain't never killed anyone in my darn life. And I ain't never visited with no prostitutes either!"

The nurse reached over to her cart and picked up first a vial of yellowish fluid and then a hypodermic syringe, which she then proceeded to fill from the vial, after cracking its top off.

When the syringe was full, she waved it threateningly at Keith. "Mr. Roche, we can do this the easy way or the hard way: Either you keep quiet of your own accord, or I'll dope you like I just did to Mrs. Harrigan."

"Okay, I'll behave," Keith said. "What's poor Mrs. Harrigan do to deserve her admittance here?"

"She killed her two children. Smothered them with pillows while they slept."

Keith gulped. "Why's the crazy woman screaming then?"

She claims the dead children come and torment her on a regular basis." The nurse's lips curved up into a cruel smile. "The doctors all think she's lying, though." Her expression turned a little unsure. "I don't believe in ghosts myself, but if she's telling the truth, I daresay it serves her right."

"And the man on the other side? What's he do ta get in here?"

"Stabbed another miner and stole his paycheck."

"How's that get you admitted to the madhouse? Ain't he supposed to have got the electric chair instead?"

"He was sentenced to the chair, but then he began screaming that the dead man kept visiting him at night, and in addition brought other dead people along with him. After a while our convict completely lost his mind. The state said it was wrong to execute a lunatic, so here he is. We'll be lobotomizing him once we're done with you. It won't cure him, but it'll definitely stop him screaming."

"Where's the darn doctor anyway?" Keith asked. "How 'bout if we just get this lobotomy over with, so's I can get on with my life?"

The nurse stared coldly at him. "Are you serious, or joking? Once your brain's been cut into, that's it for you. You'll be no better than a carrot. Are you in a hurry to experience that?"

Keith laughed and shrugged. "A life's a life. So, what if afterwards I'm a veggie? I just feel sorry for you uppity lot that's gonna have ta feed me and wipe ma backside whenever I poop myself."

The young nurse's face literally turned red. "Oh, you disgusting, disgusting man. You're just like all the others. And here I was thinking that maybe they were wrong, and that you really had nothing to do with Sammie Dean's death. But . . . but . . ."

Speechless, she whipped her body around and headed for the door of the operating theater. There, she turned to stare at Keith. "I'm going to hurry the doctor up. You know, I'm going to enjoy seeing you get yours."

Keith smirked at her. "So, what ya delayin' for then, woman? Just remember ta wipe my ass clean when it's your turn on potty duty."

The nurse angrily vanished from sight.

Once she was gone, Keith breathed a sigh of relief. Putting on that show of nonchalant machismo had been the hardest work he'd done in his life. In reality, he was utterly terrified; the thought of having his delicate artist's brain cut into was supremely scary.

Throughout the time he and the young nurse had been talking, Keith had been wriggling his left arm around, trying to loosen it enough to slip it out from beneath the tight leather strap. He'd finally felt something snap slightly. But he'd known he'd needed to get the nurse out of the room, so he could properly work his arm free; hence the nonchalant talk.

She said she's going to hurry the doctor up; which means he's currently busy with something else! That should buy me some time.

Keith quickly worked out that the easy way to free his left arm was to slide it up over his hip. This was just about possible with the strap slightly loosened like it now was. Not wasting any time, Keith got that arm free and next undid the buckle holding down his middle parts. Once both of his arms were free, he quickly undid the other two leather straps, first the one around his chest and then the one around his ankles.

Loud disjointed and insane laughter echoing from down the corridor on his right further galvanized him and gave his motions the desired urgency. Almost before the laughed ended, more mad screaming began, which was soon mixed up with the loud clanging of someone banging on his or her cell door and demanding to be let out at once. This was scary for Keith, because it probably meant the nurse would soon need her tranquilizers again.

Finally free, Keith slipped off of the gurney and stood on the floor. He didn't move for a while, waiting to be sure he was stable on his feet, as his head still throbbed so much that he was wishing he'd asked the nurse for an analgesic shot.

But she'd most likely just shoot me up with that tranquili—

Keith's eye dropped to the nurse's loaded medical cart. Lying there amidst the color riot of medicines was the loaded hypodermic that she'd threatened him with.

Smiling, Keith picked up the hypo, and then realized he done so not a moment too soon, because now he could hear footsteps approaching the operating room. He listened for a moment. As he'd expected there was more than one set of approaching footsteps.

I need to time this to perfection, he told himself, and hurried over to stand beside the door.

"Well, it's time for your operation, Mr. Roche," the nurse said with pleasure, a few seconds later. "Let's see how you enjoy it without any anesthetic!"

The young woman had already stepped into the room before realizing that Keith was no longer strapped onto the gurney.

She immediately began looking around nervously for him. However, before she turned back towards the door and saw him, Keith grabbed her from behind. He wasn't sure where to inject her with the sedative, so he just stuck the hypodermic needle into her arm, and depressed the plunger a little. He didn't want to use it all up.

She was so confused by him snatching her like that, that she made as little resistance as a rabbit. Then she turned around and looked at him in surprise and dread.

"You nasty, nasty murder!" she gasped in a shaky voice, and next began wobbling on her feet.

Behind her, a large man in a white coat was now stepping into the operating theater. Apparently, the doctor been delayed somewhere along the corridor and so hadn't seen Keith inject the nurse who'd come to fetch him. Now too, the doctor just saw that the young woman was in some sort of distress, and so he headed for her to help her out.

Keith waited until the doctor was within range, then he lunged at him and jabbed him in the left buttock with the hypodermic. He quickly depressed the plunger, and then, leaving the hypo stuck in the man's behind, he ran out of the operating theater.

***

The second that Keith made it through the doorway of the operating theater, the strangest thing happened. The air around him seemed to warp itself and he was suddenly once again someplace else.

What the fuck is happening today? he wondered in fright. He was however extremely relieved that he'd escaped from the lunatic asylum. He looked back the way he'd just come. On the other side of the door before him was the operating theater. The doctor and nurse lay on the floor, both struggling to remain awake. Keith was unsure if they could see him, though the nurse kept pointing in his direction as if she could.

Anyhow the important thing was he was no longer in that madhouse. He knew that he wasn't. The noises of the incarcerated crazy people had ceased the moment he stepped through the door.

But where am I now? Then he looked to his right and realized that somehow, this second transition had shifted him back to the Jerome Grand Hotel. He didn't even question the impossibility of this happening. After what he'd been through, it was more than enough that he'd made it back safely.

And with the transition, his clothes had again altered. The hospital gown had vanished off of him and Keith was once more wearing the clothes in which he'd set out from the hotel this morning.

Earl is gonna freak out when he hears about all this. Okay, so I'm back in the Jerome Grand, but what floor is this?

The door that Keith was standing beside still looked like a portal to another dimension. He hoped that no one would step into the corridor at the moment, because he had no way to explain what was going on.

How can I? I don't even understand it myself?

A quick look at the doorway opposite let him know that he was on the fourth floor. The hallway clock informed him the time was 3 p.m.

Okay, I'd better get Earl to come see this before it vanishes, Keith thought, and ran for the stairs.

CHAPTER 15

Earl was stretched out on his bed when someone knocked on his door.

He'd been deep in thought, worrying and also wondering where to start looking for his brother again. The knocking startled him, but he leapt up from the bed and headed for the door.

The knocking came again, insistently this time, before he reached the door.

"Must be Minnie coming to ask what progress I've made in the hunt for her darling," he grumbled as he bent his eye to the peephole.

He was very surprised to see Keith standing outside his room. He quickly opened up the door.

"Hey . . . what . . . where . . . ?"

But Keith had now grabbed his arm and was pulling him out into the third-floor corridor. "Come with me, bro, you've gotta see this before it vanishes!"

Earl was about to pull back and resume asking his questions. But two things prevented him from doing so. First of all, someone had shaved Keith's head bald. And second, Keith had a manic expression in his eyes, almost like he was high on drugs.

"Did you go to get stoned with those acid-freak artist friends of yours again?" Earl asked as Keith pulled him out into the corridor. "Nancy's gonna be so pissed about that. She's worried sick about you and I am too—"

"Just come with me, bro!"

"Okay, lemme get my shoes first!"

"No time for that. Come on!"

Earl looked back to the nightstand on which the key to his room lay, then he sighed. If Keith wasn't about to let him pull on his sneakers, there was no way he'd let him reenter the room to get his key either. "Okay, let's go see what's got you so excited," he agreed.

Leaving the door slightly ajar, he nodded to his brother. "Lead the way."

Keith had already begun running. He led Earl to the stairs. "Waiting for the elevator will take too much time," he explained as they both ran upstairs, with Earl trying not to trip up, though Keith seemed heedless to the dangers of making a misstep and ending up in freefall.

They quickly emerged on the fourth-floor landing. There was nobody in the corridor.

As the brothers burst out of the stairwell, Earl saw what had gotten Keith so worked up. One of the doors in the middle of the corridor was glowing. Moving closer to the radiance, Earl saw that the glow was being created by a foot-wide circular space, like a mirror, that was shrinking as they watched it. But there was something in the mirror. He didn't understand what he was seeing, but the mirror seemed to be reflecting the body of a woman lying on the floor. Earl was surprised by this, that he looked behind him.

"It's not a mirror—it's a fucking time portal, bro!" Keith informed him. "Somehow, while crossing that road I was flung back in time and . . ."

Earl nodded, and with this information in mind, did his best to see exactly what lay on the other side of the contracting hole. By now it had shrunk to about half of its original size, but Earl still got a good enough look to understand that he was looking at a hospital room— this had to be an operating theater—and that two people—a doctor and a nurse—were lying on the floor; both of them seemed to be unconscious.

I can only assume that at the moment I'm looking at part of the old psychiatric clinic this building once was. Keith must have knocked those two out cold. Wow, is that a hypodermic stuck in that man's behind?

While making this assessment, Earl Roche felt remarkable calm. However, his calmness was the result of his suppressing a huge amount of frustration.

Earl was still cursing the ghostly complications that prevented him from recording anything in this place, when the portal winked completely out of view.

He stared at the space where it had been for a while, and then stared at the door number.

"Room 43," he muttered to himself and then turned to give Keith his full attention. "Is that where they shaved your head?" he asked.

"What head?" Keith replied. Then he flung up a hand and rubbed it, and so discovered that he no longer had any hair on his head, just a bald scalp. "Dammit! I had no idea they'd shaved me bald." He shook his head wondrously. "I never even checked. I was too desperate to leave there before . . ."

"Before what?" Earl asked.

"They thought I was the one who killed Sammie Dean. They were gonna lobotomize me."

Earl's eyes widened. "The famous *dead* Sammie Dean, the hooker?"

Keith nodded slowly. "One and the same."

Earl mused on that. "So . . . who did kill her then?"

"Some guy with a beard like Abe Lincoln. The nurse said his name was Jonathan."

Earl had never heard of the man. He stared at the door to Room 43 again. "You know, rooming in this building just gets odder and odder." He nodded to his brother and then gestured back towards the stairs. Let's head back downstairs and go check on Minnie. She'll be delighted that you're okay. Then later, once you two lovebirds have reconciled enough, we'll have a conference in my room."

So, they made their way back downstairs again. Down on the third floor, the door to Earl's room had swung open a little wider, but nothing seemed disturbed. Leaving Keith to alert Minnie to his return, Earl entered his room to slip on a pair of sandals and also retrieve the room key.

Minnie must have been asleep in she and Keith's room, because she only opened their door after Earl was done with closing his.

"Darling, she gasped in delight and flung herself into Keith's arms. There was a few moments' kissing, and then she and Keith entered the room, with Earl following closely.

"Hey, what happened to your hair?" Minnie asked Keith when they separated. She giggled. "You do look cool like this, but I preferred your former look. And, man, you're supposed to ask your girlfriend first?"

"What on earth happened in here?" Keith asked her in disbelief, as he looked around the room. "It looks like a twister swept through here."

"Man, a twister might have done less damage." Earl too stared in shock. The hotel room was completely trashed. Everything that had been neatly arranged the last time he'd been in here (which was just this same morning) was now completely either upended, shattered to glass or ceramic shards, or else was lying disheveled somewhere. Even his cases of precious cameras, signal receivers, and spare hard drives had been affected. All of that expensive gear was mingled up in a mess of pillows and towels, cracked-off wineglass stems, Ouija boards, paperback novels and magazines . . . a strip of condoms . . . sunglasses, shoes, shirts, tangled pantyhose . . . everything laying just about anywhere where it had found space, with no pattern to the grandiose disarray.

Is that actually Minnie's hair dryer hung up on the overhead fan?

Minnie sat on the edge of the bed. Suddenly she looked very miserable. "Guys, it's a *very* long story," she told the brothers. "It all began when I finally woke up this morning. I was eating some cookies, when suddenly, these poltergeists began messing with me. . . ."

Earl and Keith listened to her strange tale with increasing disbelief.

CHAPTER 16

"The dead guy in the elevator room was Claude Harvey, generally known as Scotty," Earl said. "He was a hospital maintenance man, back when this place was a hospital. If my dates are right, he died around 1934 or so."

"Yes," Herman agreed. "That must have been him. I just couldn't remember his name earlier in the day."

"His picture is hanging on a wall somewhere here," Keith added. "I know I've seen it at least once, but I don't remember which floor it's on." The others had marveled at his story of how his head had gotten shaved. He now wore a baseball cap to cover his baldness. Minnie still thought he looked cute.

"How exactly did Claude Harvey die?" Nancy asked. She looked questioningly at Minnie.

Minnie shook her head. "I never bother to research the gory details of our cases. I always leave that nightmare-fuel stuff to the guys."

It was 8 p.m., and the five of them were gathered down in the Jerome Grand Hotel's bar again. They hadn't yet moved to a booth, but were all seated along the bar, with Riley serving them again. They had arranged themselves at the end of the bar, taking advantage of its curvature to be able to see each other clearly.

Though unstated in words, it was now understood that the five of them constituted a group of some kind, a group that had to stick together for its own wellbeing. In one sense they were bound by their sense of mystery, of having experiences things that the hotel's other guests had not. In another way, they were also bound by their feeling of terror, and by their need to resolve the mystery of what was going on around them; a mystery that had somehow now involved them in its happenings. A feeling of apprehension hung over them all, along with the sense that they were all in some sort of yet inexplicable danger, and that if they didn't quickly arrive at the root cause of all these events, there might be a terrible price to pay. What that terrible price was, none of them could have said if questioned; but the feeling was a very present one; and also, a very mutual one.

Nancy nodded to Earl. "Hey, tell us how Claude Harvey died."

Earl sipped his liquid valium. "Well, Scotty, as everyone called him, was discovered, just like you guys said you found him—head under the elevator like that. But then the story gets weird, you know."

"Weird in what way?" Nancy probed.

"Well, for one thing, other than for his broken neck, there weren't any marks on his body, just a bruise near his ear. So, how'd did he get under the elevator?"

"Suicide?" Nancy said. "Maybe he jumped."

Earl shrugged. "Some people said so. But there wasn't any evidence to back it up. His body was arranged the way you saw it down there, mostly outside the shaft. There's no way he couldn't have jumped, broken his neck in the fall and wound up ninety-five percent *outside* of the elevator shaft."

Herman's brow creased up in thought for a while and then he nodded. "Yeah, that's right. To wind up like that, he'd needed to have fallen forward on his face . . . or back."

"Exactly," Earl went on. "Other folks thought it was an accident, but Scotty was an experienced technician; so how could he have had an accident like that, and wind up lying in that position?" He sipped some more of his drink. "Which leaves the possibility of murder."

"So, *was* he murdered?" Minnie asked.

"No one's sure about that," Earl replied. "I've heard two version of events. One version says that an inquest was held—most likely here, as it was a hospital then, so why cart him off elsewhere—and it was determined that the elevator hadn't killed Claude, he'd been dead before it rested on him."

"That's weird," Nancy said. "Makes it seem like he really was murdered."

"But that's just one version of the story. The other version claims no inquest was ever held. Meaning there was no autopsy. That version also claims Scotty's death was hushed up, that a massive coverup took place."

Nancy shuddered. "That makes it seem even more like he was murdered."

Earl nodded. "My thoughts exactly. Anyway, back in the day, rumors abounded, and there was a list of potential suspects, but nonetheless Claude Harvey's death remains recorded as an accident."

"That's just so sad," Minnie said. Then she waved to get the bartender's attention. "Another glass of red wine please."

Riley nodded and approached with the wine bottle.

***

"So, are we supposed to solve the riddle of Claude Harvey's death or what?" Herman asked. "Is that what the hotel wants of us?"

"I dunno," was Earl's reply. "There's lots of reports of people seeing Claude's ghost, either in the basement, or near the elevator itself on one of the hotel floors. In most of these sightings, the ghost is said to be furious; really angry about something. It's speculated that he has some unfinished business he'd had to take care of, and is angry that now he'll never get to do it."

Herman nodded. "It's something to go on, I guess."

Herman was surprised by how quickly he'd gotten pulled into Earl's paranormal assessment of things. *It's completely unlike me to be discussing the supernatural like this, like we're disputing whose turn it is to make a beer run to the supermarket!*

But, no matter how much Herman would have loved to, he could no longer sensibly (and responsibly) doubt the existence of ghosts. He knew what he'd seen this morning.

I touched that dead guy and he felt solid enough. He wasn't an optical illusion or a projection of some sort. He was there, seemingly in the flesh, and then he suddenly wasn't there anymore. I can't deny that. And there was also how we were shifted out of the elevator. That was supernatural or miraculous or whatever.

But something bothered Herman. Riley the bartender could clearly hear what they were talking about, and yet the man showed no sign of being bothered in the least.

Maybe he's simply jaded to all this by now. I can't imagine that we're the first or even the fiftieth group of hotel guests to sit at his bar like this and speak in wonderment of our supernatural experiences. After our experience this morning, I can heartily confirm that this hotel's reputation of being haunted is very well deserved.

Then Herman's eyes narrowed. *But maybe, there's something more to this. What if Riley has inside info about this place, that he could share if he was persuaded to do so? Maybe the dude is in touch with the spooks? Maybe he can see them as clearly as we do?*

***

Keith suddenly said, "Ladies and gents, so far we've all overlooked the obvious."

"Which is?" Earl asked.

"Well, why don't we all just pack up our gear and head back to our respective homes? Once we're all away from here, we'll surely be out of any danger."

But surprisingly, it was Minnie of all people, who countered his suggestion: "Not smart, baby. I don't wanna alarm anyone, but this morning I got the clear sense that this hotel wants something from us all, and that if we don't give it what it wants, we'll all gonna regret it."

Keith sighed and spread his hands on the bar top. "But, baby, if we just leave abruptly, we can maybe trick the building into letting us go. This Jerome Grand Hotel building been here in one form or another for the past hundred-odd years. No way has it been waiting around just for us five to show up." He looked at his brother. "Earl, you're the expert on stuff like this. What do you think?"

"I dunno," Earl said. "And if I seem to be saying that a lot recently, it's because our situation keeps altering rapidly." He looked along their group of five. "Twenty-four hours ago, I'd have immediately sided with my brother's suggestion that we all simply pack up and get the hell out of Dodge." He frowned. "But now, no. Keith, feel your damn head and remember how you lost your hair. If you'd not escaped from that past version of this place, you'd be lying in an asylum room in the past, a vegetable with no memory of who you were, while here in the future, we'd all be combing the town for you."

"You know you're merely strengthening my argument that we split right away, right?" Keith asked.

Earl shook his head. "No, I'm not. I'm advising caution. Let's not piss off the hotel—or whatever paranormal agents it has monitoring us. And there may be a whole lot of them. Claude Harvey aside, about six thousand people are believed to have lost their lives here in Jerome during the great flu epidemic of 1917." Earl fell silent, as if leaving his brother to draw an obvious conclusion.

"Wow, six thousand? That's a town-load of ghosts," Nancy said.

Keith looked pleadingly from her to Herman. "Please make my brother see reason. I think we're endangering ourselves by remaining in this crazy town." He whipped off his baseball cap. "I'm living proof that these ghosts can hurt us."

"Put your damn cap back on, bro; you're becoming a celebrity in here," Earl said.

Keith looked around and saw that several of the bar patrons were now looking his way; something about his bare head seemed to rivet their gaze on it. After glaring at his brother, he put the baseball cap back on and resumed staring at Herman and Nancy.

"Strangely enough, I think I side with Minnie and Earl here," Herman said. He looked at Nancy. "What do you think?"

She nodded too. "Yeah, me too. I do believe we need to work out what's going on." She nodded to Riley and tapped her glass for a refill.

"So long that is, that none of us are in danger . . . then I'll suggest we all check out and get the hell out."

Minnie nodded. "I agree with that. So, Keith . . . baby—"

Keith wasn't done yet though. "Hey, Earl," he said in a slightly desperate voice, "we have to leave town in three days anyway. You're forgetting your vacation is coming to an end."

"Not anymore," Earl immediately retorted. "I already contacted the bank and requested an additional week's leave. I'm owed much more than that, and they readily agreed."

Everyone stared at Earl.

"When was that?" Keith asked, "We've been together all day."

"Did the internet start working when you got back to the hotel?" Minnie asked.

Earl shook his head. "Nothing dramatic like that." He smiled at Keith. "It was after you went missing. When I couldn't find you, I was desperate, so I headed for the town hall and called the bank from there. Thankfully, I arrived at the town hall during a spell when the phones were working. I also wanted to report your disappearance to the police, and get them looking for you, but no one I spoke to at the Jerome Police Department paid any attention to me."

"They must've though you were joking," Herman said. "All these small-town folk are alike; they're wary of outsiders even though they derive their living from us tourists."

"It might not have even been that," Minnie said, nudging her boyfriend with her elbow. "Remember the law says you can't make a missing person's report except the person hasn't been seen or heard from for twenty-four hours."

Keith had listened to all of this with a frown on his face. "So, we're all staying then?" he asked in a defeated voice.

"Yup, we are," Earl said.

"Yup," the three others chorused.

"Okay, I won't try to run out on you then," Keith agreed. "I'll hang around here too and we'll try to work this out together."

"Good man," Herman said appreciatively. "Okay, let's get to drinking now." He gestured to Keith's mostly untouched brandy. "Drink up, kid, and I'll buy you another."

Keith grinned and picked up his drink. He sucked some down, and nudged Minnie. "I'm sure you've other reasons for not wanting to leave town."

She began giggling, then leaned in and whispered something in his ear that cracked them both up.

"Hey, jokes are my speciality," Nancy said, then she began laughing too.

Earl stuck up a finger. "Hey, before we're all too drunk to realize what we're doing, I need to ask Nancy and Herman something: do either of you have a Polaroid camera that I can borrow? I wanted to get one sent to me from home, but the phone line cracked up right when I was about to ask for it."

"I've got one," Nancy said. "I've lots of refill cartridges for it too."

Herman stared at her. "You have a Polaroid? I thought those things were extinct."

She nodded and looked sad. "I always travel with it. Used to be my husband's. Somehow, Micah continually overwrote any photos he'd take on his cellphone. Despite being a wonderful husband and father and manager, he was clumsy with most technology, and totally craptastic with digital devices. So, whenever Micah wanted to be certain he'd actually photographed something he wanted to keep a memory of, he used the Polaroid, which he couldn't accidentally erase." She sighed and her voice turned wistful. "I've kept up the habit in his memory and now always travel with the old camera. It's upstairs in a suitcase right now." Then she looked at Earl oddly. "but what do you need such an old camera for?"

"He thinks we can record the ghosts on it," Minnie explained.

"That true?" Herman asked Earl.

"Yeah," he nodded back. "We can't capture them with modern devices, but perhaps old-school equipment might work. Anyhow it's worth a try. I'm committed to this investigation, and I need something to keep proper records of the results."

CHAPTER 17

All efforts to get Riley to say something about the hotel's suspected noncorporeal resident proved fruitless. Herman quickly began suspecting the man was being paid to say nothing.

When the taciturn man did speak, it was always in 'maybes,' as in, the Jerome Grand Hotel may or may not be haunted, and it might or might not have poltergeists. Where ghosts were concerned, the Jerome Grand Hotel's evening bartender seemed not to have any idea of actualities. This was surprising, considering all of those guest logs in the lobby that brimmed with visitors' accounts of hauntings and sightings. Those thick binders in the hotel lobby contained an exhaustive number of accounts from past visitors to the Jerome Grand Hotel, each of them swearing they'd personally encountered a disembodied spirit.

Riley was always polite and smiling, and never ignored a question from any of the drinkers, but still, Herman found the man's uncooperativeness frustrating in the extreme.

Finally, everyone put their heads together for a whispered conference, with Earl and Keith leaning in so they could hear what the middle three—Herman, Nancy, and Minnie—were saying. This conference occurred once Riley was cleaning glasses at the far end of the bar, and so wouldn't be back for a while. The black waitress serving those drinking in booths was also first noted to be out of earshot.

"I think we can now safely assume that 'stirring up a sense of mystery in the bar's patrons,' is included as part of this dude's job description," Earl whispered in disgust.

"Never before in my life have I met a dude with such a buttoned-up lip," Nancy agreed.

"We'd better retire to yesterday's corner booth," Herman responded. "Plan A hasn't worked."

'Plan A' had been the five of them sitting in earshot of the bartender and holding a discussion on paranormal topics for an hour. The idea had been to both gauge Riley's reaction to their conversation and also see if they could draw him to comment on something or other that they'd said. But that had clearly not worked out.

"So far, I don't like how this investigation's goin'," Nancy said in a slightly slurred voice.

"I agree," Minnie instantly agreed and then pointed over her shoulder. "Listen, let's reclaim our drinking booth before someone else claims it."

"Okay," Earl agreed. "You ladies go on first. We'll order fresh drinks for everyone."

Nancy and Minnie eagerly got to their feet and hurried away.

But no sooner had Minnie vacated her bar stool than a tall thin man sat down on it. Herman, Earl and Keith had been trying to catch Riley's eye again and hadn't seen the newcomer arrive, but when they turned towards him, each of them couldn't help thinking they knew him from somewhere.

The man smiled at them and then turned towards Riley, who'd just walked back their way. Riley had been heading for the trio of Herman, Earl, and Keith, but had naturally stopped in front of the newcomer first, because he was first in line.

"Hey, Mikey, how's it been?" he greeted the tall and thin man. "Been a while since I've seen you in here."

"I've been busy," the man replied with a broad smile. "I'm in town for a few days and thought to drop in at the old watering hole. So, Riley, how's thing here in the haunted hotel?"

Riley shrugged and grinned. "So, so. Nothing ever changes. I'm not really certain if we've even got any ghosts left anymore. Numbers seem to keep lessening by the year. Almost like the tourists are carting 'em off."

To Herman, Earl, and Keith, who'd hardly ever heard Riley utter more than one sentence at a time, hearing the bartender hold a normal conversation was a huge surprise. But this was nothing compared to what he did next.

Because next, Riley told the tall man: "Hey, Mikey, it's great you walking in here like this right now." Then he turned to the other three men: "These guys are good friends of mine, they're really interested in ghosts and ghost stories and such like, particularly those connected with the Jerome Grand Hotel. I'm wondering if you could take a little time to help 'em out with a few things, facts and details and such like."

"Why sure, why not?" Mikey said, and also turned towards Herman, Earl and Keith, each of whom was individually wondering if he were dreaming. "So, what you wanna know, fellas?"

"Hi, I'm Earl Roche," Earl quickly introduced himself, "and these two gentlemen with me are my brother Keith, and our good friend Herman Broderick."

Mikey extended his hand and shook hands with them all. "Glad to meet y'all. I'm Mickey Thompson. I'm a fireman, been living and working in these parts for years."

"So, what can I get all of you?" Riley asked.

"Beer for me," Mikey replied him.

"And for us too," Earl told him. "But I think the girls both want more of that sweet red wine." Then Earl smiled at the bartender. "Thanks, Riley. I owe you one."

"Don't mention it, bro," Riley grinned back. "This one's on the house."

"So, what exactly would you gentlemen like to know 'bout the ghosts in this hotel?" Mikey asked.

"A whole lot of things," Herman replied. "But first of all, let's collect our drinks and join the ladies over there. They're also very interested in hearing what you've got to say."

CHAPTER 18

"You're mostly right in your assumption," Mikey told everyone when they were all seated at the booth. "The hotel does pay Riley not to discuss the ghosts with the customers. Their policy is to let folks encounter the spooks for themselves." He sipped some beer and grinned. "But of course, those rules don't apply to us folks from town or neighboring places who don't work here, who both know the local history and have a few scary tales to tell."

Earl nodded. "Well, we've quite a scary tale of our own to tell," he said. "I wonder what you'll think when you've heard the whole of it."

"Lay it on me, I'm listenin', " the man replied.

Earl had quickly warmed to Mikey Thompson. The fireman was a down-to-earth guy, and Earl liked him. Mikey seemed to be in his mid-thirties and was craggily built, wiry and with a stubble of beard. Earl was still very certain he recognized his face from somewhere; but he couldn't say where. He was still surprised by the turnaround in their investigative fortunes. *So, Riley has been on our side all along? Well, that's good to know!*

With occasional additions from his four companions and interjected questions from their new friend, Earl quickly ran down the list of what had been happening to them in the last few days. Mikey's eyebrows quickly raised when Keith recounted what had happened to him that morning, and Minnie's account of her poltergeist visitors had them all in stitches.

After Earl was done telling his tale, he asked Mikey: "So what do you make of it all?"

"I'd say that a lot of it's familiar and a lot of it's unfamiliar," Mikey replied with a serious expression on his face. He nodded at Minnie.

"For instance, her experience is an extreme type of a normal phenomenon here. The cleaning staff tell literally hundreds of tales of spirits throwing things at 'em while they're making beds and fluffing up pillows, just nothing as violent as what happened to Minnie." Then he scowled. "But I've honestly never heard of that old elevator behaving like that before. That's something new for sure. And then, your getting magically transported out of it and then your seeing young Claude Harvey pinned dead beneath it. I've never heard of that manifestation before either. What most folks report is seeing Claude down there where he was killed, looking mad as hell about something. But no one's yet reported such a solid manifestation."

Earl looked at Herman and saw that Herman looked bothered. "You're wondering what this alteration in the way Claude's ghost shows up could possibly mean, right?" he asked Herman.

"Yeah, it's like we've somehow triggered something off by going down there. But what?"

"I'd suggest y'all don't worry your heads about it," Mikey said, tapping the top of his beer stein with his fingers. "The important thing is, none of you were harmed and you got out alive."

"Yeah, but at the time it was really scary," Minnie said. "When that old miner appeared, I almost wet myself from sheer fright."

"I think he just wanted to turn on the lights," Mikey said. "That's apparently all he ever does. Most people say—"

"Where did he die?" Herman asked. "He's not the one called Headless Charlie, is he?"

Mikey laughed. "No, no. Headless Charlie died in one of the mining tunnels under the town. They found his head but not his body, and nowadays he supposedly haunts those old mine shafts where he once worked. Ah, now that you mention it . . ."

He fell silent and looked pensive. When he said nothing for a while, Nancy said: "You look like you're remembering something sad, like really said. "What happened?"

Mikey nodded at her. "Yeah, I am. There was a mine cave in a few years back. A group of tourists were killed while on a tour of the old

Copper King mine tunnels. I was one of the firemen who pulled out their dead bodies."

He sighed. "It was just one another hot day, till we got that call. We rushed out there hoping we'd find some survivors, but no. The hillside had crumbled in on them, a delayed result of all that mine blasting they'd done in the past, the press claimed." Suddenly, the fireman looked close to tears. "Anyway, we got there too late—not that I believe arriving any earlier would have made one whit of a difference. The tourists had all been smothered by sand."

"Oh, my God, that's just horrible," Nancy said.

"Hey, I remember watching that on the news," Earl said. He did, and now it had clicked in his mind where he knew Mikey from. He'd seen Mikey that day, carrying a bloody and mangled little body over his shoulder, while trying to fend off several overly-intrusive cameramen. By Earl's reckoning, the dead kid couldn't have been more than six or eight years old.

"I've never been able to forget that day," Mikey said, wiping his eyes with the back of his hand. "I'd been at search and rescue operations before, but none of 'em ever had that kind of an impact on me. That day was just horrible. Like time had come to an end in there."

"It's okay, Mikey, we understand," Minnie said, reaching over and laying her hand on his.

The others all nodded their understanding too and Mikey slowly regained his composure. "I'm alright now," he said after a while. "It's been three years now and they've even reopened the tours to that part of the mountain."

"Is that even safe?" Minnie asked with a doubtful expression.

Mikey's expression turned thoughtful. "Well, yeah sure, I think it is. My sister Susan runs a shuttle tour service, and she told me of how much trouble they had to go through to get the county officials to agree to let them conduct any more tours in that region of the hillside. Apparently, four teams of state geologists came out here and combed the hills looking for fault lines that might trigger a repeat cave-in. But finally, the state gave 'em the all-clear and the tours resumed."

"You know, I'd like to visit the sight of that original collapse," Earl said. "Might be some residual ghostly activity out there."

Mikey scratched his chin. "Well, that particular mine shaft is closed now, but my sister Susan can take you out there, just to look around. Susan runs Phantom City Tours. Their office is three houses up from the Town Hall."

Earl mentally filed away this information. He'd look into it tomorrow. He had a sudden hunch that this was a good lead to follow up on, and he was prepared to do whatever it took to unravel this mystery.

Seeming fully recovered now, Mikey gestured over at the black waitress to give him another beer. Then he smiled at their group of five. "So, the way you've explained it to me, you guys wanna catch some of the spirits here in the hotel on camera?"

"Oh, we'd love for that to happen," Keith said nonchalantly, flipping his baseball cap backwards. He looked at Minnie who frowned and shook her head, and so he flipped the peak forward again.

"The other thing we wanna do, or rather *need* to do," Earl said, "is to get to the bottom of this mystery of why this hotel—maybe this entire town of Jerome—is picking on us today. For some reason, I feel that once we understand what the hotel wants from us, the whole matter will stop."

"Do you have any suggestions that might help?" Nancy asked Mikey.

He frowned. "Not directly, no." Then he waved a finger at them all. "But there's a time-tested method of communicating with spooks that never seems to fail."

"What's that?" Herman asked.

Mikey grinned. "Hire a psychic, what else?" He laughed at their stunned looks. "Hey, I'd have thought that's the first thing you ghosthunters would do."

"My not thinking of that myself really bothers me," Earl admitted. "I tell you people; this building really *is* messing with my mind."

He looked at Keith, but Keith had apparently already lost interest in their discussion; he was grinning and whispering into Minnie's ear, while she too, was concentrating on whatever joke he was telling her.

"I did think of us hiring a psychic, but had no idea where to look for one around here," Nancy said. "You know, with no internet and all that. All the spooky sisters I know personally live out west in Cali."

"Oh, you needn't go that far," Mikey said as the waitress placed his fresh beer in front of him. In addition to running her tour service, my sister Susan is a bonified psychic. She regularly conducts seances to contact dead people." He grinned. "She comes cheap too, 'specially when I tell she'll be doing a favor for some friends of mine."

CHAPTER 19

The time was about two a.m., when Earl, Keith and Minnie made their way down to the second floor. Not wanting to disturb any light sleepers, they descended using the stairwell beside the elevator.

Earl nodded as he stepped out into the corridor. "The coast is clear."

The others stepped through after him. At this time of night, the corridor was largely dark. The old building would have felt creepy even if one hadn't actively been searching for paranormal activity within its walls.

"Hey, what's all the cloak-and-dagger behavior for?" Minnie whispered. "It ain't like we're gonna be robbing anyone."

"No, but *they* don't know that," Earl explained. "If we disturb any of the guests on this floor before the ghost appears, they might make sufficient noise before we calm them that the ghost disappears again." He nodded to his brother. "Call the elevator and lock it here."

This part of the plan was simply more of what he'd just explained to Minnie. The old Otis self-service elevator could only be called elsewhere if its doors were shut. To ensure that this rule was understood and observed by all hotel guests, the hotel management had stuck a notice on the elevator door itself, explaining that both elevator doors needed to be closed both during and after use; the latter closure being to ensure the elevator cage didn't wind up stranded on one of the hotel floors.

So, Earl's intention now was to call the elevator to the second floor and then open its doors, both to ensure that no one could ride in and scare the ghost they were seeking away with the noise the machine made, and also to prevent those same people getting off at this floor before they were through.

"Well, your best bet is the second floor," Mikey had agreed, when Earl had laid out the framework of his plan. "That's where the old miner is most likely to appear at that time of night."

So here they were. Earl had Nancy's Polaroid camera in hand and two pockets full of spare film for it. Minnie hadn't wanted to come along, but she didn't really have any other choice. She was scared to stay in their wrecked room alone, in case the poltergeist spirits returned and possibly attempted to throw *her* around this time. She'd suggested that she sleep in Nancy's room tonight, but Keith had vetoed her suggestion.

"Hey, what's the matter?" Earl asked Keith impatiently. "What's taking you so long?"

Keith stabbed his finger on the elevator's call button again. "It's not coming, bro!" he whispered harshly. "I think it's stuck on another floor."

Earl hurried over to his brother's side and examined the empty cage. He pressed the call button a few times himself and then said, "Yeah, looks like you're right." Then he hurried away again, and snapped his fingers at Keith, gesturing to him to follow.

During a short reconnaissance trip on their way up from the bar, they'd worked out their place of concealment. This was behind an upright piano positioned opposite a fire extinguisher station. In normal lighting, the piano wouldn't hide their bodies, but with the lighting dimmed like it was now, there were sufficient shadows in the corridor that anyone looking down its length, would be unable to see the line of people crouching behind the piano. Of course, this didn't apply to anyone emerging from the two rooms on the other side of the old keyboard; but this was a calculated risk Earl considered worth taking.

So, they lined up behind the piano, Earl crouching in front with the Polaroid, Keith behind him with an audio recorder, and Minnie behind them both.

"How long is this gonna take?" Keith whispered. "I'm so tired from the day's ordeal that I don't wanna fall asleep here."

"Try to remain awake for the next hour," Earl replied. "If we don't see the ghost by then, we'll call it a night and try again tomorrow. But I'm hoping he does show, according to Mikey, there's been lots of sightings of the old miner at this time of night."

"Yeah, yeah," Keith agreed. "But I'm also thinking that anyone wandering the hotel corridors at two in the morning is liable to be drunker than the proverbial skunk and liable to mistake their own alcoholic breath for Casper the friendly ghost."

"Hey, what's the matter?" Keith said, when Minnie suddenly grabbed him tightly.

"Ca-ca-cat!" Minnie gasped. "Black cat!"

"Will you two please keep your damn voices down!" Earl pleaded in an exasperated whisper. "I don't see any damn cat arou—"

But then he did. The cat was prowling along the wall near the elevator. It must've come out of the stairwell. At first Earl didn't understand why Minnie was so scared of the beast, but then he got it, although even then he really didn't get it. It was just another cat. But at the same time, it wasn't just a cat. In some inexplicable way this seemingly innocent black feline reminded Earl of death.

Then the cat vanished into the shadows and Earl heaved a sigh of relief.

"I don't know about you, bro, but that cat just scared the crap outa me and I've no idea why," Keith said.

"I've no idea what that's about either," Earl agreed. "Maybe it's just another mystery the hotel wants us to unravel. Maybe it's like that old Edgar Allen Poe story where the murderer sealed the living cat in the wall with his murdered wife."

"Yeah, I remember that story well," Keith agreed. "The guy killed her and then—"

"Hey, fucking stop scaring me, you two!" Minnie whispered.

Earl rolled his eyes. "Hey, Minnie, if you're that scared of a silly cat, what are you gonna do when the miner shows up?" Then suddenly, at the opposite end of the hallway, one of the switched-off lights came on, and then another one did. "Oops, I think he just showed up. Minnie, don't make a peep or I swear to God I'll kill you!"

"I feel like I'm dying already!"

Earl raised the Polaroid camera and aimed it at the end of the corridor. "Please shut up! The ghost is here."

At first the ghost himself wasn't visible, but by the time the third corridor light came on, they could see him as clear as daylight. An old man with a thick scruffy beard, dressed in old clothes. There was something both pathetic and intimidating about him. Pathetic, because he clearly hadn't been either rich or in the best of health at the time of his demise; and yet he was intimidating, because, in that same decrepit condition, he now emanated a fierce negative vitality; the vitality of death.

The ghost miner moved forward along the corridor, not walking but floating over the blue-toned rug, and a fourth light came on. Earl saw that the ghost was giving each light switch the faintest of touches.

Earl suddenly realized that the temperature in the corridor had dropped; not uncomfortably, but enough to be noticeable.

"Is this the guy you saw yesterday morning?" he asked Minnie as he took his first photo.

"Yep, that's him alright," she whispered back. "Somehow, he seemed scarier then. Now he just looks like a regular old dude who needs to eat better."

"That must be because I'm here with you," Keith told her. "You know I'm gonna protect you like I'm the ghostbusters."

"Shush, both of you! We don't wanna scare him away!" Earl handed the Polaroid photograph the camera had spat out to Keith. "Wave it in the air, while I take some more. We don't know how long he's gonna hang around for."

But the ghostly old man was already fading into nothingness. Earl got just one more photograph and then the corridor was empty again.

The three of them stood up and stared at the area of the corridor where the ghost had just been. Earl was airing his second photograph.

Even if both snapshots proved unusable as evidence, he was satisfied that his efforts tonight hadn't been in vain. Now, he had good proof that the hotel was haunted. He'd seen one of its legendary resident spirits with his own eyes.

Keith pointed ahead at the ceiling lights that were slowly dimming again. "Do you think the camera flash startled him?"

Earl shook his head. "It wasn't that. As far as I can tell, he didn't notice us. He didn't flinch at all when the flash went off. And yet, for some reason, he didn't come near the eleva . . . Hush, guys, get back down! Someone's coming up the stairs!"

They ducked back down just in time. The next moment, the stairway entrance next to the elevator swung open and three men entered the corridor.

Two of the men were dressed in white laboratory coats. The third man, whom Earl and the others soon realized was being carried by the two men in white coats, was dressed in the sort of dark jumpsuit janitors and maintenance men wore. The two men in white dragged the third man to the elevator entrance, and thumbed the call button.

As expected, the elevator didn't respond.

"Looks like the dude had an accident," Earl whispered. "He seems to be out cold." Earl couldn't clearly make out their faces, but the one being supported by the other two was dangling between them like a limp noodle.

"We'd better let them know that the elevator's not coming," Minnie said.

"No need to, baby—they should be able to work that out by themselves," Keith said. "Hey, why are they opening the door to the elevator shaft if the elevator isn't coming?"

And it was true. Now, clearly smiling to themselves, the two medical men were sliding open the elevator shaft's glass door. Once it was open, one of them leaned inside and looked up, then he backed out into the corridor and nodded to his companion.

"Are they trying to work out which floor the cage is on?" Earl whispered. "Why not just carry the wounded man down the stairs?"

But then, before any of the three ghosthunters who were watching them could call out an alarm, the two medical men picked up their unconscious burden and threw him down the elevator shaft. They dumped him down head-first and then quickly slid the shaft door shut again. The men smiled and nodded to one another for a few seconds and then left again via the stairs.

Minnie gasped and began breathing heavily.

"They just murdered that guy," Earl said. "We need to call the cops."

Before the killers' departure, Earl had been worried that they might have guns and could shoot him and his companions, but now that they'd left, he felt it was necessary to raise an alarm. So, he began to rise to his feet, ready to start yelling and alerting everyone to the dastardly deed that had just been done here on the second floor. But then Earl felt a hand on his shoulder pulling him down into hiding again.

"Don't panic or shout," Keith said.

"But they just murdered that guy," Earl repeated fiercely, feeling a surge of righteous indignation. "We can't let them get away with that!"

"No, bro, they murdered that guy maybe *eighty* years ago," Keith said.

Earl turned and stared at him. Keith was nodding at him. "Yeah, bro, before they threw him down the elevator shaft, I got a good look at his face. And I recognized him from the picture they have up on the wall here somewhere. That was Claude Harvey we just saw being thrown to his death."

"For real?" Earl asked, hoping Keith was right.

Keith nodded. Minnie was holding Keith tight. "Are you sure it was Claude Harvey? If you're wrong, that guy might be lying dead at the bottom of the shaft, with a broken neck."

"Yes, it was Claude, I can positively guarantee it. All we saw was a ghostly reenactment of his murder."

Earl relaxed. He found it hard to believe, but it made sense. "So now, we know how he died," he said. "Claude was thrown to his death from this floor, and then the elevator was lowered down onto his body"

"That still doesn't explain why he lying was mostly outside of the elevator," Minnie said as they all got to their feet again.

"Oh, I'm sure those guys had it all worked out beforehand," Keith said. "After dumping the guy down the elevator shaft, I think they split up. One of them headed downstairs to arrange the body in the basement so as to confuse investigators, and the other one went upstairs to close the elevator doors, so they could call it down to the basement and flatten his head under it."

Earl nodded. "So, apparently at the beginning, they did exactly what we had planned to do; they locked the elevator in place up on either the third or fourth floor, so that no one else could use it till they'd finished murdering Claude."

Minnie shivered. "That's just evil. It's horrible to imagine what people are capable of."

"Well, we've solved the mystery of Claude Harvey's death. As to why they killed him, we'll never know the facts of . . ." And then Earl's grim expression brightened up perceptibly. "Hey, hey, hey!"

"Keep your voice down!" Minnie hissed at him. "That's what you've been telling me all night. What's gotten into you anyway?"

Earl thrust the Polaroid snapshot in his hand at her. He did lower his voice, but not by much. "Success, that's what!"

Minnie and Keith both stared at the Polaroid picture. There, unmistakable in living color, was a clear image of the ghost miner.

Earl was beside himself with joy. "Just wait until Herman and Nancy see this!" He pointed to Keith's hand, which seemed to remind Keith that he too was holding a photograph. Keith raised his own Polaroid picture to the light. It was exactly the same as Earl's, a perfect capture of the ghost miner's ghostly image, taken just as the light above him was reaching full glow.

"I daresay we three can all go to sleep now, after a hard night's work!" Earl said enthusiastically.

The others nodded their agreement. Feeling like a conquering emperor, Earl led the way over to the stairs and back up to their floor.

CHAPTER 20

Earl Roche's delight and satisfaction at having achieved his desire of capturing the old ghost miner on photographic film did not translate into a sound and refreshing night's sleep for him.

Instead, that night Earl had one of the strangest dreams of his life.

The dream went thus: Earl was sitting down at his laptop in a hotel room somewhere. He had the two Polaroid photographs of the ghost miner laid out on a small table and was trying to scan them with his cellphone. But then, a black cat entered the room. The cat first of all regarded Earl with its bright green eyes, and then it leapt up onto Earl's laptop and first shredded and then ate up both snapshots of the ghost.

Once, it was done eating the two photographs, the cat turned its attention to Earl, who was suddenly filled with terror.

And then the black cat grew larger and larger in size until it was about the size of a lion. Then it leaped on Earl, grabbed him by the throat, and dragged him outside into the corridor, where it dragged him towards the opened elevator shaft. Once there, it threw him down the elevator shaft and stood staring down at his corpse with its glittering green eyes.

Earl woke up muttering. "No, no, stop!"

He didn't return to sleep easily after that. The mystery of the black cat perplexed him. The dream cat was clearly meant to be the same black cat that he, Keith, and Minnie had encountered down in the second-floor corridor.

But what does it have to do with me? What's its connection to the three of us? Is it a familiar of this haunted hotel, a messenger of some sort?

He thought on the dream for a while, but could make no sense of it; and finally, he fell asleep again.

123

CHAPTER 21

Herman Broderick awoke feeling really good the next morning. He got out of bed, had a shower, and reflected on his plans for the day, which hinged on what everyone had decided last night before they got too drunk to make sense of anything.

Their plans were in two sections:

Firstly, because no one had wanted to drive into town in the morning, and also because Mikey would be returning home that night anyway, it had been agreed that he would contact his sister Susan for them and book a private tour of Jerome for the five of them.

However, maybe because they'd all been slowly descending into a state of drunkenness, the primary destination of the tour had been set as the old Copper King mines where Mikey had said a disaster had killed a similar group of tourists three years ago.

Herman shook his head at the memory. *How drunk we must've gotten. Why in the world would we choose to visit that ghoulish location . . . of all places? Oh yeah, it was mostly Earl's doing. He got this bug in his brain, that that old mine would be an excellent location to restart his research from, because that Headless Charlie ghost might turn up in there too. Anyway, I wish him lots of luck on his wild goose chase!*

Ghosts or no ghosts, Herman no longer cared. Viewed this morning, yesterday's load of worrisome questions about the haunted hotel's apparent interest in them seemed ridiculous to him. Even his experiences with Nancy and Minnie in the elevator seemed ridiculous to him.

But they did happen; I can't deny that. But that doesn't mean I have to get sucked up into Earl's paranormal conspiracy theory. I'm gonna let the ghosthunters

*hunt their prey . . . my main part in this is to protect Nancy. I'd hate myself if
anything happened to her!*

Earl walked out onto the balcony of his room and while looking
down at the spread of the town, considered the second part of the
day's plan.

*Okay, when we get back from the day's touring, Mikey's sister is gonna hold a
séance here tonight for us.*

He was startled out of his thoughts by the sound of Nancy stepping
out onto her own balcony on his right. He leaned forward and peeked
at her just as she did the same. They both laughed. She yawned and
gripped her head like it hurt. Then she moved over to the wall
separating the balconies.

"We really can't keep meeting like this," she said. "Either I come
over to your side of this Berlin Wall, or you'll come over to mine. Pick
one."

"Never refuse a lady," Herman said, laughing. "Get your door open;
I'll be right over."

She backed off from the balcony and Herman hurriedly retreated
into his room and put some proper clothes on. Then he hurried out
into the corridor and knocked on Nancy's door.

"Hi, sleepyhead," he said, embracing her once she'd let him inside.
"How was your night?"

"Lonely, 'cos you weren't beside me," she joked back.

Herman knew she was joking, but still, he liked the sound of it. Yes,
he too wanted to go to sleep by her side and wake up by her side.

While letting her out of his embrace, he smelt the sweet fragrance
of her blonde hair and kissed her cheek.

"Hmmm, I like that," Nancy whispered. "I could really get used to
it." Then she yawned again, took his hand in hers and gently pulled
him through her room and outside to the balcony railing again.

Once more, Herman looked over the railing, looking away from his
own balcony on Nancy's left, and instead staring towards the balcony's
right end. The wall divisions prevented him seeing the farther balcony
sections, but in the balcony section nearest to Nancy's room, he caught

a glimpse of her neighbor on that side, parking his wheelchair against the railing. Then the man sat staring down the hillside at the town. After a while, he turned and stared at Herman too.

From this angle Herman couldn't really make out the other man's face. But then, he neither needed to, nor wanted to. He'd seen the man before, outside in the corridor and knew what he looked like, and now his mind substituted that image in the place of the indistinctness. The man next door was seemingly in his middle years, but Herman couldn't be sure of that, as there had been something in his countenance that spoke of him being prematurely aged by misery. On, seeing the man's face yesterday, Herman had felt chilled by it. Never before had Herman seen such a living portrait of human suffering.

Back then in the corridor, Herman had quickly looked away from the unknown sufferer, just like he did now. But the disturbing effect of looking at the man next door must have shown on his face now too, because he saw that Nancy was staring seriously at him.

"What's the matter?" he asked her as they stood side by side.

But no, Nancy had something else entirely on her own mind. "I'm just running my mind over Earl's suggestions for today. I'm fine with us exploring the old mine, but that séance is a total no for me. Mainly because Earl wants us to hold it in the *elevator*, of all places." Her expression became really worried. "Herman, I really don't think that's a good idea at all. As it stands, I'm half-scared to even set foot in that creepy elevator cage, not to mention summoning ghosts into it too."

Herman gave her a reassuring smile. "Don't worry, I think it's a dumb idea too. When we meet the others to start the tour, we'll join forces to talk Earl out of it. I'm sure Minnie will back us up too. And Keith will likely go along with whatever Minnie wants."

Nancy nodded gratefully, and hugged Herman to her again. And Herman suddenly realized that here and now was both the right place and the right time to express his feelings to Nancy Lee, and to begin charting their shared 'happily ever after.'

"You know, Nancy . . ." he began carefully.

"Yes, Herman, what is it?" She'd begun smiling again and it made her look beautiful and melted his heart all over again like the first time they'd met twenty years ago. He knew he wanted to keep watching her smile like that for the rest of his life.

"Well, I've been meaning to talk to you about something, but the time has never seemed to be ri—" Then Herman froze. "Hey, what's that man doing? Hey, what are you doing!"

Nancy had been looking up at Herman with an expectant look in her eyes, as if she already knew what he wanted to say. But now, seeing the alarm take over his features, she spun around and looked over the edge of the metal railing and across to the next balcony section, where Herman's gaze was focused.

The miserable man in the wheelchair had somehow pulled himself up onto the railing. He was balanced like a gymnast on an exercise horse, with his body completely in the air, half on the balcony and half off of it. His intention was obvious, he was going to commit suicide by falling from the third floor to the parking lot.

"No don't!" Herman said, stretching out a hand to the man. There was no time for him to rush out of Nancy's room and try to stop what was about to happen, but Herman at least attempted to do so, carefully moving Nancy behind him and leaning as far over the railing as he dared as he signaled to the suicidal man.

"Hey, man, wait. I don't know what you've got on your mind. I don't know what's troubling you, but killing yourself really ain't a solution!"

But then the delicately balanced man turned to look at him, and smiled. And that smile—the smile of a man who'd finally found peace after an eternity of suffering—froze Herman in his tracks.

He couldn't move and felt Nancy in turn pressing against him. Together they watched the suicidal man tip his body forward over the railing. Suddenly the man was airborne, plummeting to his fatal crash. And next, just before he would have hit the ground in the parking lot and burst his head open, he blinked out of existence, and his death never occurred.

Herman blinked himself, and then quickly looked along the balcony again. The man's wheelchair had vanished too.

Herman looked at Nancy, who'd begun trembling in fear.

"So, he was just a ghost then?" she asked. "In broad daylight?"

"You know," Herman replied, with a spooked look on his face. "I now believe holding that séance is a fantastic idea—even if we do have to hold it in the elevator."

Looking equally spooked, Nancy nodded her head. "Yes, yes, yes! We must!"

The she buried her head in Herman's chest and began weeping.

Herman sighed grimly at the morning. Damn that ghost for ruining the romantic mood!

CHAPTER 22

"I wonder what the psychic will be like," Minnie said after letting him into she and Keith's room. "I've always been wary of people who claim to see what I can't."

Their room was still in a mess. Earl had already taken several Polaroid photographs of the poltergeist damage to complement his other evidence.

"Forget what she looks like," he growled at Minnie. "What you and your boyfriend need to do is get your slacker asses out of bed and into the shower. We've a long day ahead of us. First the mine and later the séance."

Earl was already dressed for the day and raring to go. It pained him that his two associates were both less than ready.

"Why don't you just go on ahead of us?" Keith asked from beneath piled bedsheets. "Dude, it's your thing, you're the main man."

"Yeah," Minnie agreed. "You're the one who kept us both up until three-thirty with your excitement over getting those pictures."

"Lady, just get in the shower and get dressed. The woman will be here any moment now!"

"You're just guessing. We don't even know if Mikey spoke to her."

Earl rolled his eyes. "Of course, Mikey would have spoken to her. They live in the same building!"

Earl waited until Keith was out of bed and in the bathroom before returning to his own hotel room. He stepped out on the balcony and, leaning forward over the railing, saw that Herman and Nancy were out there too, together. He was going to hail them, but they weren't looking his way and then they both stepped back out of view.

Earl sighed. *How come I'm the only one with any real sense of urgency about this matter that concerns all of us?*

He reentered his room, and sat brooding on his bed.

***

While sitting on his bed, Earl ran his mind back over the dream he'd had. Since waking he'd been unable to get it out of his mind. The black cat that had dumped him down the elevator shaft just like they'd noticed Claude Harvey being dumped!

Of course, Earl didn't give any real credence to dreams. He knew Sigmund Freud's theories and stuff. After last night's initial perplexed incomprehension, He'd finally worked out that he'd dreamt of the cat throwing him down the elevator shaft because he'd seen a black cat near the elevator shaft; and that sighting had become mixed up in his subconscious with his group's supernatural vision of the hospital maintenance man's death. Same went for the Polaroid pictures the cat had eaten in the dream; the same process of random association had created that dream sequence.

So, to Earl's thinking, though it had been remarkably vivid, the dream really meant nothing. But the cat . . .

The cat! A chill went through Earl each time he remembered last night's sighting of that little glossy black beast. He couldn't shake the impression that the cat had somehow signified death. And not just his own death, but all of their deaths.

But why? That was the puzzle he needed to resolve. And until Earl was able to resolve the puzzle, he wouldn't have peace of mind.

The cat . . . death . . . black cat . . . death . . . what's the connection between them? I know that black cats are considered harbingers of evil. But in this case, where will the evil occur? Will it be in the elevator? That makes sense because we noticed it near the elevator. It might be smarter to hold the séance outside the elevator, rather than inside of it. I'll need to discuss this with the others. However, I'm not telling anyone about this dream I had; or they'll really think I'm losing it.

Still troubled by vague stirrings of dread, but feeling positive that he would soon resolve the dilemma, Earl settled back on the bed, and mentally urged the others to get their shit together quickly, before Mikey's psychic sister arrived.

CHAPTER 23

Mikey's sister Susan was a female version of himself. She was tall, thin, and possessed a warm personality that instantly endeared her to everyone.

"Sorry, but my brother can't make it today 'cos of work," she explained when they met her in the hotel lobby. "But not to worry, Mikey already told me everything you want done. And I'll do my utmost to oblige you."

"Sorry if I don't look much like a psychic at the moment," Susan Thompson said once they'd all introduced themselves. "But we're first goin' out on a tour and I always reserve my spooky getup for when I get my Ouija board out."

Everyone laughed, and then after they'd discussed and agreed to her charges, Susan led them out-of-doors towards her tour bus.

***

Since their joint scare on the balcony, Herman was keeping Nancy close by his side. Or rather, she was staying glued to his side like she was scared to be on her own. Herman really liked the feel of her body against his. Since getting divorced, he'd forgotten what that felt like; having another warm body in close proximity most of the time; a body that in a sense belonged only to you, and which you could grab on the shortest of notices for comfort.

Herman and Nancy followed the tour guide to her tour bus—a 2013 GMC Savana 15-passenger van.

Herman was back in good spirits again. He'd suddenly realized that this tour into the surrounding hills which Earl had requested was actually the perfect occasion for him to hold his discussion with Nancy. She was clearly ready to hear what he had to say, and if that ghost hadn't reenacted its death right here in the parking lot, he and Nancy Lee might right now be dating properly again.

Remembering that wheelchair-ghost made Herman look upstairs at the third-floor balcony. It also brought back to his mind those creepy ghost photos Earl had taken with Nancy's camera. Wow, it had been weird seeing the old miner. Herman fully understood now why Minnie had been freaking out yesterday when they'd found her trembling in the elevator.

But it's alright now! he thought happily. *All I gotta do is, once we reach the sight of the cave-in, I'll take Nancy on a walk away from the others, and then I'll tell her of my love for her. I don't care a whit about Earl's research. He can have the mine to himself for the day!* Then Herman laughed to himself. *Besides, so long as we stay away from Earl once we reach the old mine, there's no chance of any ghosts finding us and ruining our romance!*

He and Nancy climbed into the tour bus.

***

Minnie Connors was also deep in thought as she got on the bus.

Okay, today is it then. I've got to do this today or I'm gonna go nuts with keeping the secret to myself. Somewhere along this bus tour I'm going to pull Keith aside and tell him that we're pregnant. I'm going to do it! Yes, I really am! And I need to do it this morning, before we start getting involved in any deep psychic stuff that'll completely ruin the mood. This is a lovely day, perfect for breaking the news about a baby

She smiled up at Keith, who had a bad hangover and was still holding his head. They climbed into the rear of the bus, behind Herman and Nancy.

"Hey, you okay?" Keith asked her after she'd sat down. "You're looking distracted."

She leaned close to him and whispered, "I'm just thinking of how much I love you, baby."

"I love you too," he replied and kissed her forehead.

Minnie pressed herself close against him and smiled to herself. Yes! She would break the good news to him this morning!

***

When the others were all seated, Earl got into the front of the tour bus beside Susan. The tour guide turned on her seat and smiled at him. "So, tell me, Earl: Mikey already told me you want the tour to end up at the closed Copper King mine, where they had that cave-in three years ago. But prior to our going there, what else would you like to see in the town or hereabouts? A trip down to Jerome's famous Sliding Jail maybe?"

But Earl shook his head at her. Then he looked into the rear of the bus. "Sorry, guys, but there's been a slight change of plans."

"What change of plans?" Nancy asked from the front row of rear seats.

"Yeah, Earl," Minnie added from behind Nancy.

Keith groaned. "Please, bro, don't tell me you got me out of bed for nothing this fine morning."

Herman alone said nothing. But Earl saw that he suddenly seemed very upset about something.

"No, no, no," Earl quickly went on. "The tour isn't cancelled. I just can't accompany you folks, that's all. I'm sorry, but you'll have to go on without me."

"Why not?" Herman asked. "And if you're not coming with us, why are you dressed and in the car too?"

Earl looked at Susan, who also nodded questioningly at him.

"Oh okay," he began explaining, "I'm still going to town with you all, but I need to use the internet at the public library, so I'll be getting off there."

"What do you need the internet for?"

"I wanna upload those photos of the ghost miner I took before I lose them."

"You got pictures of him?" Susan asked. "I'd really like to see them."

Earl nodded. "Sure, no problem." He tapped the bulky laptop case he had with him. "But they're packed in here now."

Susan nodded.

"That's all?" Herman asked. "That's why you're not coming?"

Earl decided to explain better. "No, it's not just that. I also want to do some online research before we hold tonight's séance. I'll explain later."

He looked at the others, hoping they understood why he was backing out.

"Hey, everyone, this might turn out to be a drag," Keith called out. "Earl's the one who set this whole trip up and now he's backing out and sending us out there on our own."

Earl rolled his eyes. He'd not expected this. Yes, he'd initially wanted to check out that old mining site, but all of a sudden, just as they'd stepped into the lobby, he'd seen a flash of black fur and black tail vanishing into the elevator. And at that moment, he'd changed his mind about going on the tour. He figured he'd be using the day better by both scanning and uploading the Polaroid photos to cloud storage (which he needed the internet for), and researching cats in association with the Jerome Grand Hotel. Only now, it looked like everyone else was about to lose interest in the bus tour too.

"Is it possible to reschedule the tour to tomorrow?" he asked Susan.

She nodded. "Yeah sure, but there'll be a charge of a hundred dollars for today's cancellation."

"Hey, don't cancel," Herman said. "Let's just go on without Earl." He looked around the bus. "Does anyone else agree with me?"

"I'm in," Minnie immediately said, then nudged Keith. "And you're in too, mister!"

"Yeah, sure, I'm in as well," Keith agreed.

Herman, Earl and Susan all looked at Nancy.

"Yeah, sure, let's go," she said. "For folks on vacation, Herman and I hardly go anywhere."

Earl heaved a sigh of relief that his pulling out of the tour hadn't ruined everyone else's day. "Okay, but please drop me off at the Town Hall first, he told Susan.

"I'll do you one better," the tour guide replied him. "You can use my office instead. My internet connection a lot more reliable than that at the Jerome Public Library and—" She laughed. "I've got better air-conditioning too."

Earl nodded. "That's great. I'll have more privacy there. Thanks."

"Don't mention it," Susan said. "It's all part of the service.

With that settled, they set off for the town."

CHAPTER 24

Susan's office was on Clark Street. After getting Earl set up in her office, the tour bus headed off towards Main Street.

The Copper King mine was actually in the opposite direction, but on the drive down from the hotel, Keith had suddenly decided he first wanted to see the town's famous Sliding Jail and take a few pictures there. The Sliding Jail lay downhill in the north of the town and they were now headed there.

"I told Earl we'd be back to pick him up for lunch," Susan told her remaining four clients as her bus made the almost hundred-and-eighty-degrees curve that put them on Main Street (which was still the same State Route 89A as Clark Street but on a slightly lower elevation). "That's included in the cost of the tour too. I'm thinking we'll eat at Bobby D's BBQ today." She glanced over her shoulder. "Any objections to that?"

Her reply was a general shake of heads.

"None, so long as the food's good," Minnie said. "Suddenly, I'm ravenously hungry."

"That's 'cos we all had liquid dinners again last night," Nancy said.

"Dunno how my liver's coping with all that drinking," Herman said. "I sincerely hope that *it is* coping with all that alcohol. I'd hate for it to quit on—"

"Hey, stop here! Right here!" Keith yelped all of a sudden.

The bus had just crossed the Jerome Avenue junction, when Keith made his exclamation. Startled by his urgency, Susan pulled hurriedly to the side of the road.

"Dammit, you scared me," she said, once she'd gotten the van safely parked beside the Jerome Town Steps and was staring coldly into the rear of her bus. "What the hell made you yell out like that?"

"Sorry, but I didn't want you to roll past it," Keith said.

"Roll past what?"

Keith pointed back at the road juncture. "That's where I supposedly vanished into thin air yesterday."

Susan's eyes narrowed. "Yeah, Mikey did mention that." She looked across the road to where Keith was pointing at, beside the Mine Museum. Then she looked back at him and she smiled. "Let's all go have a look. I'll try to see if I can pick up any psychic emanations from the spot where you vanished."

Now Keith looked worried. "What if it happens again?" He tapped his baseball cap. "Last time I got stuck in the past, I almost had brain surgery. And the cops might still be looking for me back in time."

Susan laughed. "Don't you worry 'bout that. There's no way the ghost police are gonna abduct you if you're with me." She waved a hand at the others. "Come on, everyone, out of the bus, let's go have a look-see. Thank of it as a warmup for tonight's séance."

Herman and Nancy looked at one another, said, "Why not?" and then they slid open the bus's side door and climbed down.

After everyone had disembarked, Susan parked her tour bus properly in one the spaces near the Jerome Town Steps, and then got out and joined them.

CHAPTER 25

If we're all gonna remain together like this I'll have no chance in hell of telling Keith my news, Minnie thought as their little group waited to cross the road, because several cars were driving up towards them. *Looks like I'll have to wait until we're up in the mines, and then pull Keith aside on some pretext.*

But then Minnie saw that black cat again. It was sitting ten yards away, near the south end of the Jerome Town Steps. On seeing the animal, Minnie shuddered and for a few seconds felt like fainting as the fear of death swept over her like tidal waves.

Then she rallied her courage about her. The cat was still sitting there, clearly staring at her. She stared back at it and then suddenly, she felt a connection between them. Not a friendly or pleasant connection, but the feeling that their fates were somehow intertwined.

I need to do something about that animal, she thought, stepping towards the cat without being aware of doing so.

And so, while Keith and the others crossed the road, Minnie instead walked down Main Street towards the black cat.

The cat showed no fear as she approached it. It sat still, as if waiting for Minnie. But when she was about a yard from it, it got up and walked away, continuing south. It walked off slowly down the sidewalk then paused and looked back at Minnie, then resumed walking again.

I guess that means I'm supposed to follow it somewhere, Minnie thought, this illogical conclusion making full sense to her for some reason. She looked back once at her friends. She saw that they were all standing on the opposite sidewalk, now at the head of Jerome Avenue, but hadn't noticed she'd abandoned them; and then she returned her attention to the cat, which had once more stopped moving and was watching her.

"Okay, lead me on," Minnie told the animal.

It set off again down Main Street and she resumed following it. Then it turned off the sidewalk and climbed a flight of stairs that ended at the entrance to a cream-colored building. Minnie paused momentarily at the foot of the stairs, but the cat had paused on the top landing and was clearly waiting for her to follow it inside, so she climbed the steps also.

Stepping inside the building, she discovered she was in a period reconstruction of an old whorehouse, two stories complete with a long interior balcony and side stairs leading to that upper floor. There were several of these reconstructions in Jerome, most of them, like this one, really themed restaurants designed as tourist traps. In most cases, the building itself had been a bordello in the past, and had been renovated for occupation in the modern era.

Minnie had passed beneath the signboard bearing this restaurant's name without reading it.

The restaurant was sparsely occupied. A few couples sat at tables awaiting the establishment's busty waitresses in nineteenth century 'whore attire' to serve them.

The cat was standing at the foot of the nearer of the two stairways that led up to the balcony, waiting for her. Minnie, who was by now in some form of trance, walked past the customers and waitresses without noticing them, and apparently without them noticing her too, because it was only by the slightest of degrees that she twice avoided collisions with them, both of which neither side appeared aware of.

It was uncanny.

Minnie reached the stairs and again ascended behind the cat, which had already begun climbing. And as Minnie climbed, she sensed something different about her surroundings. When she reached the top of the stairs and looked down again, she saw that the restaurant below was now full of people. Where before there had been silence and moderation, now noise and confusion reigned. The men were all half drunk and loudly calling for more wine and beer, while the waitresses hurried back and forth with beer-laden trays that they tried not to spill as the men attempted to grab them and pull them down onto their laps, or pinched and smacked their buttocks. The smell in the place ascended the stairs like a living being; the reek of unwashed bodies and the mingled odors of beer and urine and vomit.

I've fallen back into the past, Minnie realized, with a feeling of fright. *It's happened to me just like it did to Keith.* How or why this had happened made no sense to her, as Keith's own transition had occurred on the opposite side of the road, at the point her four friends would right now be examining.

Her alarm was mingled with fascination, however. The black cat was with her here too, waiting for her as before, this time at the middle of the balcony.

Minnie didn't see herself wading through the tumultuous sea of humanity down below, to once more regain the front entrance. She had no idea it would still be there anyway.

Keith said he tried to cross back to the other side, but the transition didn't reverse.

Deciding she had no other real option in the matter, Minnie resumed following the cat.

As she stepped forward onto the balcony, the smells of this upper level hit her. There was more sweat odor, but also a lot of feminine perfume and rosewater.

Up here was clearly the prostitutes' quarters. Attractive women adorned the balcony in all states of dress and undress. A number of the women were tightly corseted, with large wigs on their heads and their cheeks well rouged. Men tramped in and out of the rooms that lined the corridors.

Keeping an eye on the black cat, which began moving again when she did, Minnie threaded her way through the prostitutes and their clients.

Her way was temporarily blocked by a stocky and smelly man with an Abraham Lincoln beard. He was leaning on the balcony railing and weeping drunkenly, while two plump women attempted to comfort him.

"Oh, Sammie, Sammie!" he wept inconsolably. "I should have saved you that night. I should never have let that madman climb into yer bedroom and strangle ya ta death!"

"It's okay Mr. Jonathan," one of the prostitutes flanking him said comfortingly. "Sammie Dean's gone now, but we're still here to comfort ya."

"But Sammie was the best—the best ever!" Mr. Jonathan wailed.

Both girls laughed. "Maybe she was, but that's over now," one of them said. "And besides, Mr. Jonathan, we're both pretty great too! Now come on and play with us like you used to play with Sammie Dean, and y'all find out right quick how much fun we are in bed."

The two girls hauled the drunken man into their room and Minnie was able to walk past.

The black cat was waiting for her up ahead. She followed it past the last of the prostitutes, to a room at the far end of the balcony. It entered the room and so did she.

A woman lay on an opulent couch in the room. The woman sat up when Minnie entered. She had long brown hair, was about forty years of age, and was passably attractive. She was very well-dressed in the fashion of the day and reeked of perfume. Indeed, this whole room she sat in, which seemed to be both her office and her boudoir, reeked of perfume.

The black cat ran over to the woman and leapt up onto her lap. She stroked its head. She studied Minnie with calm green eyes.

"Who are you?" Minnie asked her. "What am I doing here?"

The brunette woman smiled. It was a cold smile, a businesswoman's smile. She continued to study Minnie, running her eyes up and down her body.

Minnie understood she was being appraised. This was also when she first realized that now, she too was attired just like this brunette woman was . . . just like the prostitutes and barmaids all were, in turn-of-the-twentieth-century female clothes.

"Who are you?" she repeated in a worried voice. "Please tell me what I'm doing here."

"My name is Jennie Bauters, and I own this fine establishment, the Mile High Inn." In contrast to her fine looks, Jennie Bauters had a gravelly voice, but one not without some charm. She also spoke with an accent that indicated she'd not always been as wealthy as she was now. "As to what you're doing here," she went on. "I asked my cat Winky"—here she patted the black cat's head and it purred affectionately at her—"to fetch you so we could have a little conversation."

Carrying her cat, Madam Jennie Bauters now got to her feet and approached Minnie.

Minnie quailed as she came closer. *It all makes sense now—I've been seeing this black cat because its owner wants to talk to me.*

She remembered vaguely who Jennie Bauters was—one of the most successful madams in the Jerome bordello scene back in its heyday as the "Wickedest City in the West." Well, the woman certainly gave off an air of opulence. And—Minnie took a quick look back out through the doorway—her brothel certainly was doing brisk business.

Minnie no longer felt bothered for her own safety. According to her recollections of Keith's experience, in this transposed state (or hallucination, though she didn't believe anyone could hallucinate such a realistic scenario as this) she wasn't in danger unless she endangered herself in some way.

All I gotta do now is keep my head until I find the doorway out of here.

"What's it ya want to talk to me 'bout?" she asked, surprised by the sudden alteration in her voice.

Jennie Bauters had reached her now. Instead of replying Minnie, she first walked around her. Minnie could feel the woman's gaze stripping her naked.

Finally, Madam Bauters stepped back in front of Minnie. "Smile, she told Minnie.

Minnie smiled. Jennie smiled back. "That's good. Your teeth are all in good condition. And your figure is equally good, though you'll be considered a little too skinny for some tastes. Still, you're certain to be a hit with my male patrons."

"What's this all 'bout?" Minnie asked, although she already had a good idea.

Jennie Bauters smiled some more. "I'd have thought that would be obvious by now. I had my cat Winky fetch you to me because I want to offer you employment in my establishment."

"What?"

"An establishment like mine is always on the lookout for the most beautiful young women," Jennie said, now returning to her couch and taking her seat again. "As I'm certain you've noticed, the Mile High Inn ain't the only place catering to lonely gentlemen in this town."

Minnie nodded dumbly. *Oh, wow. This ghost woman wants to hire me to work as a prostitute. Frigging fantastic.*

"I'm in competition with several other madams," Jennie Bauters went on, while stroking Winky. "We're constantly on the lookout for fresh talent, and so I had to snatch you up before"—her expression soured a little—"Nora Brown sees you, for instance."

"Nora Brown?" Minnie pretended innocence. "Who's she?"

"A nobody who thinks she's somebody." Jennie stopped speaking and performed the unladylike action of spitting on the rug, then went on in an angry voice: "She tells everyone who'll listen that she's the one who got me started in this business of ours, but . . ." Then she regained control of her temper again and smiled broadly at Minnie. "But let's forget her for the moment, shall we? For the moment, let's concentrate on business: Now, girl, you're a young and a pretty one for sure. Your name's Minnie, isn't it? Minnie Connors?"

"Yes, ma'am."

Jennie smiled again. "Now, Minnie, how would you like to work for me here at the Mile High Inn? I'm sure you saw some of my young ladies on the balcony on your way here. They ain't sufferin' and business is boomin'. So what'cha say?"

Bearing in mind that being polite was in her own best interests, Minnie replied. "Well, ma'am Jennie, I ain't sure I can handle that kinda work. I'm a delicate type of girl and I don't know that I can handle all that kinda pawing from men I don't even know. It seems kinda dirty, you know. What with my uncle Toby bein' a preacher man and always talkin' about what's right in the sight of God and his glorious angels."

Jennie Bauters laughed. "Oh, that's nothing to worry about." She gestured down her exquisitely clothed body. "I wasn't always this full-figured myself, ya know. When I started, I was the original string-bean, and didn't imagine I'd survive that kinda rough male usage either. But it was easy enough. Now, I will admit that the boys from the mines get a l'il bit rowdy at times, but you'll come to no harm for sure. All you need do is examine each man's member before he sticks it in and—"

"But, ma'am Jennie, I cain't be no whore," Minnie blurted out, unable to help herself. "I'm preggered, and I love the man who's knocked me up, an' I wanna marry him an' be a good wife to him!"

Minnie was surprised at her own outburst, but the emotional pressure had been building in her for days now and the valve had to leak somewhere.

Jennie Bauters nodded. "Yes, girl, I thought you'd say that if I tried to hire you, but I thought it worth a try anyway."

Minnie gave her a shrewd look. "Then ya don't wanna hire me no more, ma'am Jennie?" It seemed odd to be let off of the hook so easily.

There has to be a catch somewhere in this, for sure.

The madam smiled. "I do want to, and maybe I still will hire you. Just not now."

"Why not, ma'am Jennie?"

"Because, Minnie . . ." Madam Jennie Bauters sighed and shooed Winky away from her. The cat leapt down from her lap, rubbed itself against Minnie's legs for a second and then darted out through the door.

"Because, you ain't never gonna be a mother, Minnie," Madam Bauters said once her cat had left the room. "I can see a few things in the future and one of them is that you'll never have a child to suckle."

Minnie gaped at her. "But I'm preggered up right now, ma'am Jennie. How comes you'se saying I'll never have a baby to look after?"

Madam Jennie Bauters' smile now had a lot of sadness in it. "That's all I know, Minnie. "Try as hard as you like, you'll never be a mother."

Minnie burst into tears. She didn't intend to cry here in front of this strange woman, who wished to sell her like a side of pork in a butcher shop, but the tears broke through her staunch emotional defenses and came pouring from her eyes.

The madam's words were so cruel, that Minnie felt the woman was placing a curse on her, one that would ensure she never carried her baby to term.

And so, she was surprised to feel Jennie Bauters' hands on her shoulders. She looked up into the woman's gray eyes and saw sympathy there.

"Come now, girl, don't cry so," the brunette said. "There's some things in life can't be helped. This is just one of 'em. I ain't a mother myself and I can't say I'm regretting it."

"Please, I wanna go home!" Minnie wept.

"And you shall," Jennie told her. "But dry your eyes first. I don't want any of my working girls thinking I've whipped you in here."

With the promise of freedom from this horrible time-trap offered to her, Minnie quickly dried her eyes on the sleeves of her dress, then she looked expectantly at Jennie Bauters.

"There, you look a lot better now, girl," Jennie said approvingly. "Okay, now you're gonna be leavin' me, Minnie. But I'm askin' that you remember my offer. I still wanna hire you to work for me here at Mile High. If you accept, I think you'll be one of my best girls, and in a short while, you'll be a very rich girl too. I can offer you a much better life than that young man of yours can. So, I'm hopin' you'll soon come to your senses and forget him and come enjoy the good life with me."

Minnie nodded. "Okay, I'll remember that, ma'am Jennie. So, how'm I gonna get out of here?"

Jennie Bauters pointed to the door. "Same way you came in. Just descend the stairs and you'll be right back where you started from."

"Thanks!" Minnie turned and rushed out of the door.

The balcony was just as crowded as before. But thankfully, this time Minnie saw no sign of the black cat. As she navigated her way between the perfumed prostitutes and their drunken patrons, she heard human grunting and bedspring noises coming from those rooms whose doors were shut.

The carnal sounds caused Minnie's face to twist up in disgust.

Myself, work as a prostitute? Damn, that woman has some nerve!

Minnie reached the end of the landing, turned and hurried downstairs. Unlike the first time, however, the transition forward in time didn't happen on the stairs. But she knew it was coming. And she still saw no sign of the black cat, which she considered a good omen.

Ahead of her at the foot of the stairs, there waited the mob of carousers and barmaids. Down there the party was in full swing, with the hall full of people, and Minnie, seeing as she'd not been shifted in time while descending the steps, now wondered how in the hell she would ever manage to push her way through the mob of people, to reach the front door and regain her freedom from this past life.

I've no choice but to run the gauntlet, she told herself firmly. *They can't flatten me.*

She stepped down off of the bottom step and immediately found herself stepping outside into sunlight again.

She felt instant relief at being in her own time again. And then she realized that instead of being returned to her exact point of departure on Main Street, she'd been transported to the other side of the road. She was standing behind Keith at the upper Jerome Avenue corner, beside the Mine Museum. Keith was explaining to their psychic tour guide exactly how it had felt to be flung into the past.

In fact, everyone was concentrating so hard on Keith's explanation that, just as they'd not noticed her departure for yesterday, none of them had noticed her arrival back into today.

Minnie didn't care. She decided to tell Keith and Earl about her experience later in the day. Then she grabbed a tight hold of Keith from behind and hugged him tightly. Thankfully, he'd just rounded up his explanation and was able to hug her back.

And holding Keith close was exactly what Minnie Connors felt she needed now. Because, even though she was back in the modern-day version of Jerome, Arizona, she still felt very vulnerable, particularly when she recalled what Madam Jennie Bauters had said about her never becoming a mother.

As much as she would have loved to, Minnie found the brothel owner's statement impossible to ignore. Jennie's words had put a total damper on her enthusiasm to tell Keith about their forthcoming baby.

Why bother, she thought with tears in her eyes that she made sure he couldn't see, *when I'm surely about to have a miscarriage?*

Then Minnie looked across the road, saw Jennie Bauters' black cat sitting on the opposite sidewalk again, and just managed to keep herself from fainting, particularly when the cat suddenly vanished into thin air.

CHAPTER 26

So far, Earl Roche had been having good success working in Susan's Phantom City Tours office. He was seated in a quiet nook away from the receptionist's desk and so wasn't being bothered by anyone who walked in to inquire about booking a tour.

The single time that Earl had required the receptionist's assistance was when he'd needed to scan his two Polaroid pictures of the ghost miner. He tried doing it on his phone, but disliked the results, and so asked if he could use the office scanner instead.

Once this was done and the results saved to a USB drive, Earl had returned to his work desk and successfully uploaded the pictures to cloud storage. Susan had been right; here in her tour office the internet was fantastic; nothing like up at the hotel; or seemingly everywhere else in Jerome. Earl had not yet made any phone calls, but the cellphone itself showed a full complement of signal bars. This disparity with the rest of the town puzzled him.

Well, that's that, Earl thought as he slipped the original pictures into the side pocket of his laptop bag, *I can't lose them anymore. Say tomorrow or so, I'll begin work on a proper writeup on our stay at the Jerome Grand.*

Earl wondered how the others were getting along with the tour. Susan had said there was quite a lot to see up at the site of the mine cave-in, and also that the area was picturesque.

Okay, now let's get some research done. I need to find out a little bit more about that old Otis elevator they've got at the Jerome Grand Hotel before we hold our séance. In particular, I wanna find out anyone has ever tried to exorcise the elevator. But that is certain to take a long time. Let me first have a look at that mine disaster three years ago that Mikey mentioned.

He ran a 'Copper King mine collapse' search on Google and found several media links. He clicked on the topmost of them and began reading.

"Yesterday, the 14th of May 2019, one of the tunnels of the now disused Copper King mine in Jerome, Arizona, which for the past decade has been open to the public as a tourist venue, suddenly collapsed, burying a tour party of nine men, women and children . . ."

Wincing at the horrible imagery of broken bodies that the article brought to his mind, Earl skimmed down to a video newsreel, and played it a low volume. The newsreel showed the mine in the aftermath of the collapse, with heavy machinery brought in to recover the bodies of the dead, and several scenes of firemen emerging from the wreckage, three of them with tears in their eyes as they carried out the broken bodies of little children.

Earl felt uneasy, but watched on.

Next in the video was the list of the dead, along with their pictures. Earl studied the faces of the victims. None of them was anyone he knew. He relaxed. He'd had the irrational fear that he would find himself listed among the victims.

That's just crazy, dude. You know that's impossible. Be sane, don't start losing it now. For God's sake, don't begin entertaining crazy fantasies.

But Earl was still in for a shock, because the video newsreel hadn't finished playing yet.

"Also among the dead is fireman Michael Thompson. Thompson didn't die in the cave-in, but instead became a casualty during the retrieval of the bodies, when a cable snapped and . . ."

Earl sat there frozen in his chair. The video was showing a photograph of Mikey Thompson, their tour guide's brother. Earl froze the video at Mikey's image and stared at it in horror.

He was a ghost? But that makes no sense at all.

Earl slowly got a hold of himself again. *No no, of course, it makes sense. If Mikey's a ghost, Susan can see him because she's a psychic. Her gift means she'd be able to converse with him like in real life.*

But this understanding now raised a further question in Earl's mind: *But then . . . how come the rest of us could see him too? And Riley too. Riley is as flesh and blood as I am; and yet, he was talking to Mikey like they were old friends and even introduced us to him, and then we all sat drinking and laughing together.*

Once again perplexed, Earl resumed playing the newsreel, which flashed Mikey's photograph on the screen for a further second before moving on to another news bulletin.

"And in a seemingly related incident, also yesterday and also in the town of Jerome, Arizona, a tour bus operated by the Phantom City Tour Company was involved in a fatal accident on the Route 89A highway. According to two eyewitnesses who were in a car in the approaching lane, the tour bus, which was being driven by Miss Susan Thompson, sister of dead fireman Michael Thompson, suddenly veered off the highway and rolled down the hillside. All five of the passengers in the bus were killed, except for Miss Thompson, who survived, but with serious injuries, including a broken leg, ruptured spleen and several broken ribs. She is however expected to make a full recovery. A number of people have already commented on the eerie coincidence of both the brother and sister Thompson siblings being involved in fatal accidents on the same day, and apparently at the same time . . ."

But Earl was no longer listening. Because now, the newsreel was showing the photographs of the five people who'd died in that bus crash three years ago.

Earl felt like he was going crazy. He froze the picture and stared at it. The top three shots of the crash victims showed himself, his brother Keith, and also Minnie. Beneath their pictures were those of Nancy Lee and Herman Broderick.

"This can't be true," Earl said, shoving the laptop away from him like it was a poisonous snake. "It's not true. I'm not dead! I'm not a ghost!"

"But it is true, Earl," a voice said nearby. "You *are* dead. You've been dead for three years now."

Earl looked at the speaker, and saw that it was Karen, the Phantom City Tours' receptionist, who was addressing him. She pulled up a chair to his desk and sat beside him.

"What do you mean, I've been dead for three years?" he demanded from her. "That's nonsense. We're both sitting her alive, you and I."

"Are we?" Karen smiled at him. The receptionist was a small, compact woman in her fifties, with auburn hair that was beginning to turn gray.

"Some ghosts don't know they're dead," she said, before Earl could reply to her question. You and your friends fit into that category."

"This is bullshit," Earl growled and then pushed back his chair and towered threateningly over the little woman. "Stop telling me nonsense!"

"Okay, if you say so," Karen agreed. "But sit down, Earl, and once you're done sitting down again, place your hand against the top of the table and press down on it hard."

Earl sat down and did as she'd instructed. Pressing down on the tabletop, he first felt a moment's resistance and then his hand popped through the top of the table and emerged from its underside. This was so surprising to Earl that he ducked his head beneath the table to look at his fingers wagging on its underside. That done he sat back up again and stared at the receptionist in stunned silence.

"Are you convinced now?" she asked. "If you're not certain what the results might be, you can try that experiment again—in fact I recommend that you try walking through the wall behind you."

Half convinced by her matter-of-fact voice, but still needing further conviction of the impossibility of what she was saying, Earl pulled his hand out of the table, got to his feet again, and walked over to the wall. This time it was much easier, he popped through the wall as if the barrier only existed in his imagination; and suddenly he was in the office behind, surrounded by Susan Thompson's shelves of books on the occult. He turned around, walked back through the wall, and once again sat down at the desk.

"Are you convinced now?" Karen asked.

Earl shook his head in a daze. "Please, tell me it ain't true." But he realized that it was true. "Hey, can everyone see me?" He asked as Karen got to her feet."

"Those of us who are psychic can." An elderly couple pushed through the doors of the office then, and the receptionist got to her feet, saying as she gestured at the elderly pair, "They, for instance, can't see you, but I can. Listen, I have to go attend to them, but I'll be back to answer any further questions you have. But in the meantime, do some thinking. Lots of things that earlier didn't make sense now will. But first off, I suggest that you check out today's date."

Earl nodded. He felt so lost at sea that he'd have danced naked outside the building if she'd suggested that doing so would help him regain his sense of perspective. While Karen walked over to attend to the elderly pair now waiting at her reception desk, Earl pulled his laptop close again, tapped on its screen, and checked today's date. 14th of May. That sounded familiar and he immediately understood why: today was the exact anniversary of the car crash in which he'd supposedly died.

His head full of questions, he looked over at the receptionist, but she was still attending to her clients. So, as she'd instructed him to do, he thought back over the past week or so. (He had no idea exactly how long he, Keith, and Minnie had been in Jerome, but it suddenly seemed like forever.)

Certain things immediately made sense to Earl. He now understood that there was no problem with the internet and telecoms signals in Jerome in general, and in the Grand Hotel in particular. Yes, all of their devices had malfunctioned because of the interference of nearby paranormal presences, but *he and his companions* were the ghosts causing those malfunctions. Meaning the TVs, telephones and cellphones were being scrambled by their presence nearby, which explained how he could be standing next to someone making a phone call and still be unable to use his own phone.

Apparently, the phones and internet work normally in here because Susan is a psychic and likely has something set up in here that neutralizes the effects of supernatural presences.

Even though he didn't understand how he seemed so solid, he also understood how yesterday, Minnie, Herman, and Nancy had wound up in the elevator room at the rear of the lobby. The elevator hadn't needed to transport them through space; the sheer shock of their crash-landing in the lobby had flung the three of them back through its walls.

Earl also now understood why he and the others always seemed to meet up in the bar, just to drink. They never went to the restaurant to eat; and they always woke up the next morning with hangovers, but hardly ever felt hungry. And if they did feel hungry, that desire soon faded. They hardly used the bathroom either.

So, their desire for food and drink and their excretory function were more the results of their memories of things they used to do, than any actual physical requirement. The reason why they kept meeting to drink was because even ghosts felt the need to socialize.

There was also the question of entering and leaving rooms to consider. How many times had he, Keith, or Minnie actually opened the doors to their rooms? Now that Earl thought on it, he couldn't tell. It seemed he remembered holding his key . . . but then, he was suddenly always inside the room anyway, and so assumed he'd walked into it. But what if he hadn't? Or had he actually opened doors and shut them behind him?

How much of my current existence is illusion and how much is real? he pondered. It was a terrifying question. *How much of what I think has happened in the past three days is merely the construct of my imagination?*

When he and Keith had had breakfast yesterday, had they really eaten, or had they imagined they had, their minds replaying a sequence of a breakfast they'd consumed in here back when they were still alive? If they were dead, how much of what they were currently experiencing were simply shared memory flashbacks of what they had all done when they'd been alive during that fatal vacation which had brought them here to Jerome? Was their current existence little more than that? Recycled memories?

But . . . I looked down from my room this morning and saw our van parked in the Jerome Grand Hotel lot . . . I see it every fucking morning when I look over my balcony. Or was I simply seeing the image of it parked there in the past? Was I hallucinating? Am I schizophrenic? I'm going crazy! Yes, I must be going crazy! Karen lied to me! I'm not dead! I'm not dead!

Before Earl's puzzlement drove him fully out of his mind, the receptionist was back in her chair by his side.

"What is happening today?" Earl groaned; his mind felt as fragile as glass and threatened to fracture into little shards of insanity. "Why has everyone insisted on going to the site of the cave-in?"

Karen pointed outside the window beside her. A black cat was sitting there watching them attentively.

"I think it's wondering why you aren't in the tour bus with them," Karen said. "You should be, you know."

Earl nodded without understanding; all he understood was that he was going mad.

"I'm not dead!" he began muttering, trying to hold his mind together. "No, I'm not dead at all! I'm not frigging dead!"

"Stop lying to yourself," the receptionist advised him in an amused voice, and then she got up and returned to her desk.

But all Earl could think of were the green eyes of the black cat at the window, and how his mind was shredding to bits from the unbelievability of everything.

CHAPTER 27

The tour bus was traveling up the hillside towards the Copper King mine.

"Well, I'm fine with holding the séance in the elevator," Susan was telling Herman over her shoulder. "I don't think you need to worry about it acting up at all."

"Umm, okay, if you say so," Herman said.

"No, Herman," Nancy Lee objected. "I'd still feel much safer if we—oh, my God, watch out!"

Minnie and Keith yelled out warnings too. A black cat had just run into the middle of the road.

Susan, who'd been expecting just that to happen, hit the brakes as hard as she could. No way did she want a repeat performance of three years ago, when she'd gone tumbling down the hillside in her tour bus. Sure, she'd been the lone survivor of that disaster, but she'd not been fit to work again for three months.

But this time she'd timed it perfectly, simply hitting the brakes and not attempting to swerve around the black cat like she'd mistakenly done the last time, when she had miscalculated her angles, which had resulted in her bus's right-hand wheels losing their purchase on the road, and had sent the tour bus first skidding and then somersaulting down the hillside.

The cat meowed loudly in fright as it vanished beneath the bus—but it was a ghost after all, had been a ghost even at the time of the accident—and so it wouldn't be hurt.

But Susan's ghostly passengers didn't know that, and had begun screaming in fright in fear of a car crash. And in a surprising replay of what had happened to them five years ago, all four of them were flung out through the walls of her bus and cast down the side of the hill.

Susan watched open-mouthed as Herman, Nancy, Keith and Minnie all went flying through the air and fell away out of her sight. All of them were still screaming in terror and at least two people were shouting prayers out to God.

Susan hadn't expected that to happen at all and so was very shocked. She'd thought she'd still end up driving the ghosts to the camp site and back again. But there they went, jerked out of her tour bus by a supernatural force and thrown downhill.

She got out of the bus and went to stand by the side of the hill, looking down at where the accident had dropped the ghosts.

Yes, there were four bodies down there, all of which suddenly vanished as if they'd never existed.

Sighing, Susan Thompson climbed back into her bus, carefully turned it around, and then headed back towards town.

Looks like we won't be holding tonight's séance in the elevator after all, she thought.

CHAPTER 28

Earl Roche was sitting nursing a beer at the bar in the Jerome Grand Hotel, when the woman sat down next to him.

Merely from curiosity, Earl looked her over. She was a middle-aged blonde, a well-preserved fifty years old or slightly older. She was well-dressed too. Earl studied her hands and didn't see any wedding ring.

Looking at the woman took Earl's mind off of his own thoughts:

Last night Earl Roche had dreamed that he was dead. He could not remember the details of the dream, just that he'd been told he was dead and he had wound up going crazy because he'd known that the witch who'd told him he was deceased had been lying to him. This evil witch had had a black cat too; he was very certain of it.

Now, Earl was a rational fellow and as such didn't give any real credence to dreams, but this one had been so vivid, almost like real life happening to him. He could still see the witch's face as she calmly informed him that he was really a corpse.

Earl laughed and sipped his beer and then considered his surroundings. He wondered how the human subconscious came up with such dream nonsense. This building was supposedly haunted, however; and maybe those creepy tales were influencing his thinking.

Meanwhile, Riley, the taciturn bartender had walked over to attend to the woman seated beside Earl.

"Hello, Mrs. Lee," Riley greeted her with a cool smile. "It's a delight to have the funniest woman in Arizona visiting our small town of Jerome, and staying at this hotel too. What can I get you to drink?"

"I'll have one of those liquid valium things you guys are so proud of," she replied, while the gears of recognition clicked into place in Earl's slightly tipsy brain.

Wow, I'm sitting next to a genuine celebrity! he realized, and began wondering how to introduce himself to her. *Keith and Minnie are never gonna believe this!*

It was an upturn for Earl, who along with his brother Keith and Keith's girlfriend Minnie, formed the ghost-hunting unit called Paranormal Research Brothers. The trio were here on Earl's vacation, but so far, had been having no luck whatsoever with capturing any spooks on film. It was crazy, that despite this hotel's huge reputation as one of the most haunted buildings in the entire state of Arizona, the most Earl had so far noticed had been cat footprints on his bed.

Okay, and yes, once the bathroom door may or may not have opened by itself. He'd been drunk at the time and so wasn't sure.

But suddenly, the ghost-hunting business looked about to take a turn for the better. Earl had an inexplicable feeling that Nancy Lee's arrival here at the Jerome Grand Hotel presaged an upswing in his fortunes in this regard.

After a look around the bar room, Earl attempted a conversation with Nancy Lee.

"Good evening, Mrs. Lee," he said as non-nerdly as he could manage. "Wow, it really is you! I've been a huge fan of yours for ages now and it's great to finally meet you in person."

She smiled back at him. "It's great to meet you too, Mr. . . . ?"

"Earl Roche, ma'am, but please just call me Earl."

"Pleased to meet you, Earl. Please, just call me Nancy, not ma'am, or Mrs. Lee. Calling me Mrs. Lee makes me feel as old as Nancy Reagan." She laughed. "You know, people often mistake the two of us."

Earl laughed too.

Nancy Lee smiled as Riley placed her drink in front of her. "So, Earl, I keep hearing stories that this building is full of ghosts. What do *you* think about this hotel's haunted reputation? Is it real, or simply another scam intended to extract money from our already over-taxed pockets? One of the reasons why I'm asking, is that last night I had a really weird dream—I don't remember it clearly now, but it was something about a car crash on a hillside. Maybe the hotel ghosts are influencing my dreams?"

Earl laughed. This was better than he'd expected. "Well, as a matter of fact, Nancy, paranormal investigations such as this just happen to be my specialty. . . ."

***

As Herman Broderick entered the bar of the Jerome Grand Hotel to meet up with Nancy Lee, he was struck by the feeling of having entered this same bar before and under exactly similar circumstances; it was a strange kind of déjà vu, as if one was replaying a previously lived life. But then, the feeling of familiarity faded as he remembered last night's dream in which he'd died in a car crash. Herman sighed. Dumb dreams—dying in that car crash had seemed familiar too, as if it had happened to him before.

He laughed. Really? So then, how many times could one die?

As Herman strolled over to the bar where Nancy Lee was laughingly conversing with a bearded man, he pondered on the best time and best place—and it had to be somewhere both romantic and forever memorable—to tell her that he still loved her . . .

***

Up on the third floor of the Jerome Grand Hotel, Minnie Connors had just awoken from a horrible nightmare. In her dream she'd been flung out of a speeding vehicle and had fallen down a hillside to her death. The dream had been so vivid, almost as vivid as real life, but she only remembered her fall, not what had led up to it.

She forced the dream from her mind; dreams were silly. She needed to concentrate on a real problem she had, here in the real world. Minnie Connors wondered how to tell her boyfriend Keith that she was pregnant with their baby . . .

***

Earl's brother Keith was standing out on the balcony of Earl's hotel room and staring down at their parked blue van. He was trying to understand the weird and tragic dream he'd had last night:

If you died in a dream, and in that dream it seemed like you'd already died in a previous dream that you'd had within that same dream, wouldn't that mean that one's dream life was a loop?

Or does it mean that my waking life is a loop? What a stupid thought!

Keith quickly dismissed the 'stupid thought' from his mind. Because for a few scary seconds, the 'stupid thought' had been so worrisome that he'd imagined it was the truth.

The End.

ABOUT THE AUTHOR

Gary Lee Vincent was born in Clarksburg, West Virginia and is an accomplished author, musician, actor, producer, director and entrepreneur. In 2010, his horror novel *Darkened Hills* was selected as 2010 Book of the Year winner by *Foreword Reviews Magazine* and became the pilot novel for *DARKENED - THE WEST VIRGINIA VAMPIRE SERIES*, that encompasses the novels *Darkened Hills, Darkened Hollows, Darkened Waters, Darkened Souls, Darkened Minds* and *Darkened Destinies*.

He has also authored the bizarro thriller *Passageway*, a tribute to H.P. Lovecraft, *When the Bedposts Shake*, an erotic horror, *THE BLACK CIRCLE CHRONICLES*, a five-part mini-series that includes the books, *Prove Your Love, Strange New Powers, Night Wings, Sheep Amongst Wolves*, and *Lord of the Birds*.

Gary co-authored the novel *Belly Timber* with John Russo, Solon Tsangaras, Dustin Kay and Ken Wallace, and co-authored the novel *Attack of the Melonheads* with Bob Gray and Solon Tsangaras.

As an actor, Gary has appeared in over a hundred feature films, including *Faded Memories, Midnight,* and *My Uncle John is a Zombie,* and multiple television series, including *House of Cards*, *Mindhunter*, *The Walking Dead*, and *Stranger Things*.

As a director, Gary got his directorial debut with *A Promise to Astrid*. He has also directed the films *Desk Clerk*, *Dispatched*, *Midnight*, *Godsend*, *Strange Friends*, and *Shoulder Down: Road to Redemption*.

OTHER GREAT TITLES FROM

Burning Bulb

PUBLISHING

WWW.BURNINGBULBPUBLISHING.COM

"Lots of action!" — Kimberly Bennett
Author, *Twisted Delights*

GARY LEE VINCENT

PASSAGEWAY

"This is a book that will keep you intrigued to the very end!"
—Christine Soltis, Author *Final Moon*

IMPOUND

GARY LEE VINCENT

GARY LEE VINCENT'S
DARKENED
THE WEST VIRGINIA VAMPIRE SERIES

DARKENED HILLS

When evil descends on a small West Virginia town, who will survive?

Jonathan did not start out his life to become a rambler, it justworked out that way. William was a troubled youth with something to hide. Both were from Melas, a small town tucked away in the West Virginia hills... a town where disappearances are happening more and more frequently.

After the suicide of a wanted serial killer, the townsfolk thought the nightmare was over. But when a centuries-old vampire is discovered they find out the hard way it's just getting started. Dark secrets can only stay hidden for so long and when the devil comes to collect, there will be hell to pay. Can Jonathan and William find a way to stop the vampire before it's too late? Find out in *Darkened Hills!*

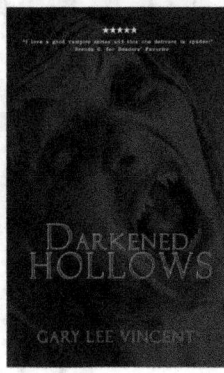

DARKENED HOLLOWS

In the heart-stopping sequel to the award-winning *Darkened Hills*, Jonathan and William must return to West Virginia to face possible criminal charges stemming from their last visit to the damned town of Melas, where both had narrowly escaped the clutches of a vampire seethe.

And as livestock start mysteriously getting murdered with all of their blood drained, worried farmers are searching for answers - leaving the local Sheriff and his deputy racing against time to learn the cause before a more violent crime is committed.

Burning Bulb
PUBLISHING

WWW.DARKENEDHILLS.COM

GARY LEE VINCENT'S
DARKENED
THE WEST VIRGINIA VAMPIRE SERIES

DARKENED WATERS

When the world goes to hell, the chosen must arise!

As Talman Cane orchestrates a flood of epic proportions in this third installment of the *Darkened* series the towns of Melas and Tarklin are caught completely off guard by the deluge. Hell-bent on finishing what they started, the evil brothers return to the lunatic asylum to take care of the witnesses and add to the ever-growing army of the undead.

Aided by Lucifer himself and the insane vampire demon Legion, the stage is set to channel all of the forces of hell to come forth. In an all-out race to survive, Jonathan, William, and Amanda soon discover they are up against impossible odds as Lucifer opens the Gateway to Hell, ushering in the zombie apocalypse and the End Times.

Find out who will survive this cosmic battle of the ages in *Darkened Waters*!

DARKENED SOULS

Melas and the Madison House are about to be rebuilt.
True evil is about to be reborne!

Young ex-priest and vampire-killer William is drawn back to the West Virginian town that almost killed him, where his vampire arch-enemy Victor Rothenstein still stalks the earth.

The town of Melas lies destroyed after the battle of the End of Days. But why is wealthy Jackie Nixon so eager to rebuild it using the bone dust of murdered souls?

Terrible evil has visited before, but the Gateway to Hell is about to be reopened in a horrific climax. And this time – it's personal.

WWW.DARKENEDHILLS.COM

Burning Bulb

GARY LEE VINCENT'S
DARKENED
THE WEST VIRGINIA VAMPIRE SERIES

DARKENED MINDS

Jackie Nixon intends to become Vampire Queen, but at what blood-drenched cost?

In this continuation to the explosive infernal saga begun in Darkened Souls, newly-turned vampire Jackie Nixon is taking no prisoners. Accompanied by her daughter, Kate, and by the captive vampire lord Victor Rothenstein, Jackie Nixon explores the Darkness. There, she intends to rouse the slumbering vampire race, bound under an ancient curse, and with their help, rule the human world.

But there's a deadly threat to Jackie's plans. Not just William who is trying to stop her, but her own royal ambitions. If Jackie performs the ritual to wake the sleeping vampires the wrong way, she could instead free the Red Beast of Hell, an unspeakable evil that even the undead fear.

DARKENED DESTINIES

With over 45 people missing after Jackie Nixon's party, the mysteries surrounding Melas and the Madison House keep getting darker.

Now, with legions of vampires at her command, can anything or anyone stop her from gaining complete control over all mankind?

The final battle has begun! As the Vampire Queen ascends her throne and sets to unleash the full forces of darkness, the fate of all things good hangs in the balance.

www.DarkenedHills.com

WHEN THE BEDPOSTS SHAKE

An Erotic Terror

GARY LEE VINCENT

STRANGE
FRIENDS

GARY LEE VINCENT

PROVE YOUR LOVE

GARY LEE VINCENT

STRANGE NEW
POWERS

THE BLACK CIRCLE CHRONICLES - BOOK 2

GARY LEE VINCENT

NIGHT WINGS

THE BLACK CIRCLE CHRONICLES - BOOK 3

GARY LEE VINCENT

SHEEP AMONGST
WOLVES

THE BLACK CIRCLE CHRONICLES - BOOK 4

GARY LEE VINCENT

LORD OF THE
BIRDS
THE BLACK CIRCLE CHRONICLES - BOOK 5
GARY LEE VINCENT

From the Creator of DARKENED HILLS...

RIVER
A VAMPIRE'S NIGHTMARE

GARY LEE VINCENT

A Vampire's Nightmare Continues . . .

RIVER

BOOK **2** ICARUS

GARY LEE VINCENT

THE
BLIND
MELODY

GARY LEE VINCENT